Wicked Tales
by Ed Wicke

Louis

fra

Ed Wicke

Other books by Ed Wicke:

Akayzia Adams and the Masterdragon's Secret
Akayzia Adams and the Mirrors Of Darkness
Mattie and the Highwaymen
Bullies
Nicklus
The Muselings
Screeps

Ed Wicke

Wicked Tales

BlacknBlue Press UK

Wicked

WHAT'S INSIDE...

Tales

You'll believe a horse can fly. But not dance.

We bears don't like hoomun fairy tales an' has our own versions. Dis one is about a cool bear who eats all duh porridge... an' duh honey... an' duh sugar. Of course.

NEVER run away from home. If you do, this is what will happen.

If a furry grey creature with beautiful yellow eyes, perfect manners and sharp teeth invites you to dinner, you really ought to go, right?

It's a real jungle out there. A little gorilla would have to be ultra-cool just to survive the journey to school.

For Rachel, Robert and Alice: who taught me how to tell stories.

Published by BlacknBlue Press UK
13 Dellands, Overton, Hampshire, England
blacknbluepress@hotmail.com

Printed in Great Britain by:
Lightning Source
6 Precedent Drive, Rooksley, Milton Keynes MK13 8PR, England

Note to the reader:

I've included a guide to the voices for anyone who isn't sure what a character should sound like. However, these are only *my* ideas, and there's no reason why the gorilla in your head should sound like the one in mine...

Alicroc the Alien

The voices

Alicroc is cool, calm and talks like an American hippy. He's so smooth and charming that you don't even notice the 272 fine white teeth, the green skin or the spiky tail. He talks in that laid-back but upbeat way that makes you think he's completely in control of the situation, even when he hasn't the slightest idea what he's doing. Which is most of the time.

The Head Teacher is a lazy slob who got into teaching by mistake. His voice is a small-town businessman's slow drawl, and it isn't helped by the fact that his mouth is full of fried chicken. You can be sure that he listens to country & western music, and would wear a cowboy hat if he could find one big enough for his head. He has food stains down the front of all his shirts.

The **Children** have so many voices that I couldn't possibly list them all. Some of them speak in whispers, some of them can't stop themselves from shouting everything, some of them cry whenever they hear the name "Mrs Wilson". Half of them lisp Alicroc's name as Alley-cwoc. Some sound like your little sister or brother, if you have one. They all sound like they would very quickly drive you mad.

The **Chickens** don't say anything. But if they did, they would sound like chickens.

The story

Once upon a time, there was an alien named Alicroc who had green, crackly skin and 272 fine white teeth. They were very sharp teeth, too. So sharp that he never bothered with a can opener. Just toss the can into the air, catch it in the mouth and –
CRRRUNCH.

He came down to earth in his black Alienmobile and decided to find a job. Unfortunately, every job he tried went wrong, and all because he didn't know the difference between Right and Wrong.

For instance, he worked the till at a supermarket but kept swallowing loaves of bread at the checkout … and tins of beans… bottles of squash… light bulbs… and any pets that wandered past.

After this, Alicroc was driving around town in his sleek black Alienmobile when he saw a sign outside a nursery school. The sign read:

**URGENTLY NEED TEACHER
FOR 4 YEAR OLDS. APPLY WITHIN.**

Now, Alicroc didn't know what a nursery school was, or what a teacher did, but he was sure he could handle 4 year olds – whatever *they* were. So he went inside.

The Headteacher was a big man with a tummy like a basketball. He was sitting at a desk, happily eating fried chicken. A lot of fried chicken, from a large, greasy bag.

'Mr Alicroc,' he said, 'I don't like you, because you're a funny colour. But I need a new teacher like a chicken needs crispy batter. Since Mrs Wilson… uh… *left*, we've had 10 replacement teachers in 10 weeks. The children simply tear them to pieces.'

Alicroc exclaimed, 'Heyyyy - these kids have got good teeth, have they? And they *like to bite*?'

'No. I mean they go on and on about how good Mrs Wilson was, until they drive the poor teacher wild. It's your turn to suffer. You start tomorrow.'

'That's Galactic!' said Alicroc. 'Hyperspace! But tell me, Headteacher: what do I *do* with all these children?'

The Headteacher took a big bite of chicken wing.

'Mr Alicroc,' he said, 'you gotta remember something: children are like chickens.'

'I see… you mean, they're *finger lickin' good*?'

The Headteacher stared at Alicroc, and a chunk of crispy batter fell into his lap.

'No, Mr Alicroc. I mean they don't know anything. Not *ANYTHING*! They're as stupid as chickens! So you've gotta explain things to them. Show them… um… Things. Tell them Things. Whatever.'

He added, 'Now get out of my office, green boy. I got some serious eatin' to do.'

So for the next week Alicroc the Alien told the children "Things". He didn't know anything about the Earth so he told them about his own planet instead.

For instance, he told them the world was shaped like a big doughnut with a hole in the middle. 'Kids!' he said, 'You gotta watch out for that hole when you go swimming! Know what I mean?'

And he told them that in the oceans there lived a kind of underwater donkey which ran around on the surface of the ocean, but upside down, with its little hooves just poking up out of the water.

They believed him. And of course they told all this to their parents at home. And their parents sent them to bed early for making up stories…

The kids all loved Mr Alicroc. But they were always pestering him about Mrs Wilson. One day a boy put his hand up and said,

'Mr Alley-cwoc, when our old teacher was here, Mrs Will-son, before she had – ' (he whispered) '- *her accident*, she let us do Painting.'

'Yeah,' shouted another. 'We did finger-painting!'
'We put our fingers in paint –'
'An' we wiggled them –'
'Wiggle wiggle wiggle wiggle…'
'And made pwetty patterns –'
'Wiggle wiggle wiggle wiggle…'
'On little bits of paper, it was fun!'
'But it didn't taste nice…'
'Why don't *you* do fun things, Mr Alley-cwoc?'
'Wiggle wiggle –'
'KIDS!' cried Alicroc. 'Kids, you just leave it to old Alicroc. I'll do something even *better*!'

So that night he went to the shops with his Inter Galactic Credit Card and bought:
✋ Four bathtubs
✋ Ten enormous rolls of paper bigger than you are
✋ Bucketfuls of red, yellow, blue and black paint

And when the children came in the next morning, there were great long strips of paper laid out on the floor, and each bathtub was filled with a different colour paint.

And Alicroc said, 'Okay, kids! Mrs Wilson let you do finger painting. But *I'm* gonna let you do:
BODY PAINTING!'
The children all cheered.
'What you do, kids, is jump into one of the bathtubs full of paint – you can keep your clothes on or take 'em off, whichever you like. And when you've got yourselves all covered in paint, you roll on the paper and sort of squidge it all about and make a

good pattern. Then you try a different bathtub, and another, and so on...'

The parents weren't pleased when their children came home covered in paint. But they WERE pleased a few weeks later, when Alicroc entered the paintings in a competition, and WON.

However, the Headteacher wasn't pleased at all. He called Alicroc to his office and said, while gnawing on a chicken bone:

'Mr Alicroc, you're still green and I still don't like you. And you're setting a bad example to the children.'

He shook the bone at Alicroc and said, 'You gotta remember that children are like chickens. They have to be kept in their places!'

'I *see*... you mean we have to put them in cages?'

The Headteacher dropped his chicken bone. 'No, Mr Alicroc. I mean you can't just let them do whatever they want to do. That's like asking a chicken to do a handstand. You *know* it's gonna go wrong.'

Things went smoothly for a while, and Alicroc managed to teach them some Useful Facts from his own world, such as:

⬆ Green water runs uphill

⬇ Blue water runs downhill

💣 Red water can explode for no reason at all

'Kids – let me tell you: never drink red water. And don't drink green water unless you're standing on your head!'

But one day, one of the children said:

'Mr Alley-cwoc, when our old teacher was here, Mrs Will-son, *before that BAD THING happened to her*, she let us do Moosic.'

'Yeah,' said another. 'We made music noises!'

'We got things to shake and –'

'Shake shake shake shake …'

'And things to jingle –'

'Jingle jingle jingle…'

'And things to hit, it was fun!'

'Hit hit hit -'

'No, that was when she let us do fightings…'

'Why don't *you* do fun things, Mr Alley-cwoc?'

'Hit hit hit jingle shake shake -'

'KIDS!' cried Alicroc. 'Kids, old Alicroc'll do something even *better*! Trust me!'

So that night he went to the shops with his Inter Galactic Credit Card and bought:

🎵 Ten saxophones, one for each child

🕐 Ten alarm clocks

And when the children came in the next morning, he said, 'Kids, Mrs Wilson let you play about with horrible bits of metal and wood. But old Alicroc is gonna teach you how to play… the saxophone!'

'Hooray! Hooray!'

So he spent all day teaching them how to play the saxophone. And when they were getting ready to go home, he said,

'Kids! You were great today. You were *astronomical*! But the only way to learn the saxophone properly is this: you gotta hide your saxophones in your bedrooms. Then you set your little alarm clocks to go off at exactly 3 o'clock in the morning. That's when you get up and – this is the important bit – LOCK YOUR DOORS!'

'Then you do exactly one hour of saxophone practice. Kids, if your parents knock on your door, you gotta ignore 'em. If they shout at you, you gotta play *even louder*. This is MUSIC. It's IMPORTANT!'

The parents weren't very pleased with being woken up at 3 o'clock every morning by the sound of a saxophone squawking. But they *were* pleased a month later, when the children were entered in a music competition, and WON.

Things were quiet for a while, and Alicroc was able to teach them more Useful Things, such as:

'Kids! The clouds are the best hiding place ever! Whenever you see big clouds go across the sky, you can be sure there's a spaceship up there, drifting along inside the clouds and no one ever noticing it… Believe me, kids: I *know*.'

But the quiet days didn't last. One day a boy said:

'Mr Alley-cwoc, when our old teacher was here, Mrs Will-son, *before she got stuck in that terrible thing,* she let us do Cooking.'

'Yeah,' said another. 'We made cookies!'

'We got eggses and flour and sugar and –'

'An' we mixed them –'

'Mix mix mix mix mix mix…'

'And made pwetty shapes –'

'Mix mix mix mix mix mix…'

'And cooked them, it was fun!'

'And they tasted *disgusting*!'

'Why don't *you* do fun things, Mr Alley-cwoc?'

'Mix mix mix -'

'KIDS!' cried Alicroc. 'Kids, I'll do something even *better*! Just tell me what you want to cook.'

'I want to cook worms, Mr Alicroc.'

'No, not worms.'

'Waaahh…'

'Stop crying, or I'll cook *you*.'

'Can we cook ice cream, Mr Alley-cwoc?'

'You can't cook ice cream!'

'My mother does. It goes all… melted.'

'Then your mother's *stupid*. Kids, I know: we'll cook spaghetti! We'll make the best and spiciest spa-ghetti ever tasted in the galaxy!'

So that night he went to the shops with his Inter Galactic Credit Card and bought:

- Four huge saucepans
- Twenty kilos of meat
- Five kilos of onions
- A dozen bulbs of garlic + a dozen chilli peppers
- Bucketfuls of tomatoes
- Every packet of spaghetti in the shop

And all morning the children chopped and cooked, and chopped some more and cooked some more, and chopped some more and put bandages on their fingers where they'd almost chopped them off.

And then they ate and ate and ate until they were stuffed full of the wonderful, spicy spaghetti.

And there was so much left over that they fed the rest of the school on spaghetti.

There were still buckets of the stuff left, so they got their buckets from the sandpit and filled them up. They took the buckets to the old people's home, and the old people stuffed themselves full of spaghetti.

And they walked down the street and knocked on car windows and said:

'Have some spetti – sgetti – smanetti!' and threw spaghetti in through the windows.

And they gave it to passers-by, and to stray dogs, and fed it to pigeons until they were too fat to fly. And there was STILL some left, so Alicroc said:

'Kids, it's wrong to waste food. So you gotta take it home with you. Put it in your little pockets and take it back to your mummies and daddies and your little brothers and sisters and guinea pigs.'

So they stuffed their pockets full of spaghetti and took it home with them.

The parents weren't pleased. And the Headteacher wasn't pleased either. He called Alicroc to his office and said, while eating a chicken sandwich:

'Mr Alicroc, you're even greener than last month and so I like you even less. Look how much of your own money you've wasted making this spaghetti!

Mr Alicroc, you gotta understand something: feeding children is like feeding chickens!'

'I *see*… you mean they ought to eat worms?'

'No, Mr Alicroc. I mean, if you let a chicken eat whatever it wanted to eat, what would you have?'

'A happy chicken?'

'NO, Mr Alicroc. You would have a poor chicken farmer! You see, I KNOW about this. I keep chickens at home. And I give them only what they *need* to have! They get Crunchy Chicken Mix once a day! They don't like it much, but it's cheap and it's GOOD for them.'

The Headteacher had another bite of fried chicken and added, with his mouth full:

'And when they're a few months old – *Scrrrch!*' He drew one finger across his neck.

'*Scrrrch?*'

'Yes, Mr Alicroc. I chop off their heads and fry them and eat them.'

'Oh… you eat their *heads*?'

'I eat the *chickens*. This is your last chance, Alicroc. Keep those kids under control, or else – *Scrrrch!*'

'I see… you mean you'll chop *their* heads off?'

'NO, Mr Alicroc. But I'll chop your name off the list of teachers!'

So Alicroc the Alien was well-behaved for a while, until one day a boy said:

'Mr Alley-cwoc, when our old teacher was here, Mrs Will-son, before she *fell into the Headteacher's chicken plucking machine*, she let us bring our toys to school.'

'Yeah,' said another. 'We brought teddies!'

'An' dollies –'

'An' my machine gun –'

'Bang bang bang bang…'

'He – *waah* - shot my teddy, Mr Alicroc –'

'I brought my toy mouse…'

'Why don't *you* do fun things, Mr Alley-cwoc?'

'Bang bang –'

'KIDS!' cried Alicroc. 'Kids, old Alicroc'll do something even *better*! Mrs Wilson let you bring your toys to school, but I'll let you bring your PETS to school!'

'Hooray!'

'Yeah, bring your little fishies, your miceys, your doggies, your kitties and your poisonous snakeys. We'll have PETS DAY!'

Now, the Headteacher learned about Pets Day and thought it was a good idea. He even said he would bring along his chickens for the children to see.

'But if you don't take care of those chickens, Mr Alicroc, you know what will happen, don't you?'

Alicroc drew a long green finger across his thick green neck. 'You mean *Scrrrch*, sir?'

'Worse than that, Mr Alicroc. I mean *somebody else* might fall into my chicken-plucking machine…'

Pets Day arrived and so did the pets: kitties, doggies, goldfish, mice, rats, snakes, two snails and even a shire horse. *And* the Headteacher's chickens.

The children had a wonderful morning, and so did the pets. But then it was lunchtime and all the children went to have their lunch while Alicroc looked after the animals….

Bad mistake.

Alicroc didn't know the difference between Right and Wrong.

And he was an Alien.

And he hadn't eaten for a month, so he had a big appetite.

He kept looking at all those delicious animals and licking his lips, looking at the mouth-watering kitties, the chewy puppies, tasty goldfish and crunchy little white mice, and licking his lips again….

When the children came back into the room, they looked all around. Then they asked:

'Mr Alicroc, where's my pet snake?'

'Mr Alley-cwoc, where's my kittycat?'

'Where's my little mousey?'

'Where's my shire horse?!!'

And Alicroc looked at the children very sadly and said: 'Kids, you gotta understand. Sometimes an Alien's gotta do what an Alien's gotta do. And sometimes an Alien gets hungry…'

'Mr Alicroc, you *didn't* eat our pets!'

'You ate my tortoise!'

'My goldfish!'

'My monkey!'

'My shire horse!'

Alicroc opened the door to the next classroom and said, 'Kids, I *wanted* to. They looked soooo tasty! But even though I don't know the difference between Right and Wrong, kids, I knew you'd be sad. So I moved 'em next door. That way, I wouldn't feel hungry from looking at 'em. See – here they are!'

And the children all ran inside and threw their arms around their dear pets. But one little girl looked all about the room and asked:

'Mr Alicroc, where's the Headteacher's chickens?'

Alicroc shook his head sadly. 'Ah…. Kids – sometimes an Alien's gotta do what an Alien's gotta do. And besides, they were *finger-lickin' good*!'

'Oh no!'

'You'll have to run, Mr Alley-cwoc!'

'You'll be put in the chicken-plucking machine like our other teacher, Mrs Wilson!'

Just then, the Headteacher opened the classroom door and asked, 'Mr Alicroc, are you taking good care of my chickens?'

'Um… I have taken care of the – *burp!* - chickens,' said Alicroc.

'Well, I hope they were good chickens today…'

'They were *very* good, Headteacher.'

The Headteacher added, 'And if they don't come back to me with every feather in place, and a smile on their little chicken faces, you children know what will happen, don't you?'

'Yes, Headteacher,' the children all chorused. '*Scrrrch!*' And they drew their little fingers across their little necks.

'Exactly. Bring my chickens to the office please, Mr Alicroc.'

As soon as the Headteacher left the room, Alicroc opened a window and climbed out. All the children climbed out too, and followed him to his long black

Alienmobile.

Alicroc pressed a button on his Intergalactic wrist-watch and the top of the car opened like the jaws of an enormous black crocodile.

'Goodbye, kids,' he said as he climbed inside. 'It was hypergalactically supercool to meet you.'

'We'll miss you, Mr Alley-cwoc!'

'You were the best teacher ever!'

'Even better than Mrs Will-son!'

A little tear ran down Alicroc's green, scaly cheek, and he said, 'Thanks, kids. That means a lot to me.'

'But Mr Alicroc, what shall we tell the Headteacher about his chickens?'

'Tell him – tell him I've taken the chickens to a better place, kids. Bye now.'

He pressed a button in the Alienmobile and the top closed again. He pressed another button and the whole vehicle tipped up – *NeeNeeNeeNeeNee* - until it was pointing straight up towards the distant stars.

He leaned out the window and said:

'See you later, kids. Be good for old Alicroc till I come back, right?'

Then he closed the window and pressed a button. The Alienmobile shot up into the sky like a big black crocodile rocket.

And as the children watched him go, they said:

'He wasn't human, was he?'

'No, he wasn't.'

'He was an Alien!'

'Just like Mrs Wilson... '

The Thundertroll

The voices

All Trolls talk gruffly.

The Littlest Thundertroll thinks very slowly. He talks the way he thinks, as if he's building each sentence out of a handful of rocks. He's a good-natured and amusing square-shaped creature who gets into all sorts of trouble by accident.

The King of the Thundertrolls is a jolly green giant who speaks with a posh accent. He's like one of those distant uncles you meet at family weddings, who pats you on the head and talks at you very loudly, as if you're deaf. His first words are usually "Goodness! Haven't you grown!"

The Thundertroll Fairy talks like an American gangster.

The Old Lady is really a young witch but she does quite a good 'sweet old lady' impression. She sounds just like your favourite grandmother, though she probably thwacks people with her umbrella more often than your grandmother does.

Rover the dog growls from time to time in a disgruntled manner. He's a small, brownish mutt who hates it when the witch ties pretty ribbons on him. What he really wants is to become a Wonder Dog and save the world from bad cats.

The Shopkeepers and Librarian talk rather severely and bossily to the Thundertroll, as they do to everyone under the age of sixty-five.

The story

You may think that thunder and lightning are made by electricity in the clouds....

YOU'RE WRONG.

Thunder and lightning are made by special trolls that live up in the sky. And this is a story about one of them, the littlest Thundertroll.

He was useless at making lightning. Every day he worked hard shaping little lightning bolts, testing them for sharpness and hotness with the tip of his finger *(OUCH!)*. But they never worked properly.

Good lightning bolts, like the ones his father made, were supposed to go

ZING
    ZING
ZOING
   ZAP!

But his own lightning al-
ways went something like

ZING
   Zinnn
zizzz
  pffff...

One morning, a storm blew up and the littlest Thundertroll took his place in the thunderclouds next to his father. And the King of the Thundertrolls came and stood next to him.

Now, the littlest Thundertroll probably just about comes up to your shoulder. But the King of the Thundertrolls is about the height of a house.

The King had a big, booming voice and was one of those jolly adults who always pat children on the head. He was doing it now.

'HOW ARE YOU? COME TO THROW SOME SPARKLERS, HAVE YOU? HO HO HO!'

(*pat pat pat*)

The Thundertroll tried to hide but got patted on the head so hard that he was shooshed down through the clouds with each pat and bounced back up again, like an apple being bobbed into the water.

'Stupid old man!' he muttered.

The King of the Thundertroll threw his first bolt, and it went

ZING!   ZAP!   **KAPOWIE!**
… and blew off a hilltop.

The littlest Thundertroll took out *his* first bolt and threw it with all his might, and it went

FIZZ Pzzz splut…

The King of the Thundertroll laughed at him. 'NOT VERY GOOD AT THIS, ARE YOU?' he roared. 'HO HO HO! HAR HAR HAR!'

(*pat pat pat*)

The littlest Thundertroll gave up in disgust and went to see the Thundertroll Fairy. He walked along the cloud hallways until he came to the Thundertroll Fairy's door. He knocked.

'Go away!' growled a deep voice.

The littlest Thundertroll said, 'But please... I'm the littlest Thundertroll and I need to talk to you!'

'Don't care! Trog off, little troll!'

But the Thundertroll was desperate, so he kicked the door down and went inside.

Now, ordinary fairies are cute. They have tiny wings and sweet little faces and dainty feet.

Not the Thundertroll Fairy. He was shaped like a very large refrigerator with a big, lumpy head attached. And instead of wings, he had a small propeller stuck on the top of his head.

When the littlest Thundertroll kicked the door down, the Thundertroll Fairy was sitting on an old settee with holes in it, eating garlic flavoured popcorn, drinking beer and watching Troll Wrestling on television.

'*Waddya want, short stuff?*' he growled.

'Please, Thundertroll Fairy, I want you to do a spell for me so I can make lightning bolts that go KAPOWIE and not phlut.'

'*Nah. I'm busy.*'

'Oh, please! I'll do *anything!*'

The Thundertroll Fairy looked at the littlest Thundertroll. '*Hmmmm,*' he said, thinking hard. And the propeller on the top of his head started going round, to keep his brain cool while he thought.

'*Orl right,*' he said finally. '*You go down to that Human-land place and get me a BIGGG box of chocolates.*'

'How do I do that?'

'*Dunno. But don't come back till you've got one. Now go away! I'm a busy fairy, I got lots of TV to watch. And put my door back together!*'

An Excursion down to Human-Land

The littlest Thundertroll waited until the next storm, and stood as usual next to his father. When his father threw his first lightning bolt, the littlest Thundertroll jumped onto it and slid down it all the way to the ground.

He landed in a gloomy bus shelter, on the foot of an old lady.

'Is that you, Rover?' she asked. 'Is that my little doggie?'

'No. I'm a troll.'

'Oh. How did you fall in a hole?'

(*Note: The Thundertroll couldn't speak Human very well, and Humans were always misunderstanding him*).

'I'm *not* in a hole!'

'Then you shouldn't have said you were! You young people are SO RUDE!' And she hit him on the head with her umbrella.

THWACK!

'Ouch!'

The old lady said, 'Look what you've done to my umbrella! You've bent it, you BAD boy. Take that! And that! And that!' She hit him several more times.

'Ouch!'

'Ouch!'

'Ouch!'

'You're as bad (*thwack!*) as my little doggie! He's run away again. *Bad* Rover!' said the old lady. 'Maybe he's fallen down the same hole as you...'

The Sad Truth

Now, I said she was an old lady. This is not true. She was actually a young witch who had turned herself into an old lady for the day. And why was she at a bus stop? She was there *pretending* to be an old lady so she could catch a nice little child to eat.

And why was her doggie there? Because little children like to stroke little doggies, and when they bent down to give Rover a pat, she would give them a push and they would end up in her huge shopping bag, upside down, with their feet poking out of the top. And they were never seen again...

And why did Rover keep running away? Because Rover was a kind-hearted creature and didn't want to be a witch's dog.

The Thundertroll repeated, 'I'm not in a hole. I'm a

troll.'

The Witch said, 'I'd help you out of the hole, but there's something on my foot.'

'It's me.'

'No, it's not a bee, dear, they're ever so small. How did you end up on my foot?'

'I slid down a lightning bolt.'

'Did you call me an old dolt? You young people!' (*Thwack* went the umbrella again. *Thwack thwack thwack.*)

'What's that smell?' she asked suddenly, her umbrella paused in midair.

'It's me.'

Thwack!

'You smell just like my dog... my dear little doggie who ran away. Will you help me look for him? I know - you could look in my lovely big shopping bag. That's right, bend right over, have a good look inside…'

She gave the Thundertroll a shove and he fell into the bag. But since trolls are very heavy, he also fell right through the bottom of it.

'You got a big hole in your bag, lady,' he said as he stood up again.

'Ohhhh!' And she hit him with the umbrella again. 'Stupid boy!' she shouted. 'Go away!'

'I can't. I've got to find a bigggg box of chocolates.'

'Well, why didn't you say so? If you want a book about chocolates, you should go to the library and ask for one.'

'Uhhhh… How do I get to the library?'

'You haven't asked politely, have you? Aren't you

forgetting the little word with the big meaning?'

'Uhhhh.... Little word with big meaning... I got it – chocolate!'

'No! You're a very stupid little boy.'

'Thank you!'

'I won't tell you the way to the library until you say please.'

'Okay....'

...After a minute the lady asked, 'Well, are you going to say it?'

'Say what?'

'Please!'

'Please what?'

'Please how do I get to the library?'

'But I don't know how to get to the library, that's why I'm asking *you!*'

'You - idiot!!'

Thwack thwack thwack.

So the Thundertroll wandered about, asking people where the library was. Some people were helpful. Others just stared at him.

This is not surprising. He was short and square.

And green.
And totally naked.

Finally he found the library and walked up to the front desk. He said loudly:

'I'm looking for a biggg –'

'Shhhhh!' exclaimed the lady librarian sitting at the desk. 'We don't have pigs here.'

'I'm not a pig. I'm a troll.'

'If you're *cold*, put a jacket on. Why are you dressed up in those funny green clothes, anyway?'

'I don't wear clothes. That's my skin...'

'Oh. You're – you're *naked*!' she gasped.

'Yes. Nice, isn't it? Do *you* like being naked?'

'What happened to your clothes?'

'Mummy never gave me none.'

'You can't come in here without clothes!'

'But I need a bigggg –'

'All right, all right! Stop shouting about your pig. Where are your library tickets?'

'Mummy never gave me none.'

'I'll have to make out a new card for you, then... Here we are... Now, where do you live?'

'Up there!!' he said, pointing upwards.

'Don't be silly, there's no one living on the roof.' She wrote something on the card. 'I'll just put down that you don't know where you live. What's your name?'

'Mummy never gave me one.'

'Don't be silly, everyone's got a name. What's your mother's name?'

'Uh... I know that one! It's "Mummy"!'

'You're a very stupid little boy.'

'Thank you!'

She wrote "Stupid Boy" on the card. 'You'll find books about chocolate in the Cooking section,' she said. 'Here, these are your library tickets. Enjoy.'

The Thundertroll took the tickets and licked one.

'Thank you very much!' he said. 'Not as nice as a box of chocolates, though...' And he wandered off between the rows of books.

He found some books like Charlie and the Chocolate Factory and started walking out with them. But the librarian stopped him.

She asked, 'Where are you going?'

'Up there!' He pointed at the clouds floating above the window.

'Don't be silly. What have you got in your hand?'

'Books. I couldn't find a box of chocolates.'

'This is a *library*. We don't have chocolate. You'd have to go to a chocolate shop for that.'

'Oh.... Thank you.' The Thundertroll started to walk out again.

'Come back!'

He turned around and returned slowly. 'Yes?'

'You need to check the books out. Where are your library tickets?'

'I haven't got them no more. I ate them.... They were very good. You got any more?'

'You can't take books out without library tickets. I NEED to stamp the tickets!'

'Oh, I still got the tickets - in here!!' He pointed at his large, green, naked tummy.

'But – but – I need to – I need to –'

The Thundertroll snatched the librarian's rubber stamp and stamped his tummy with it.

'There. You done it now. Bye!' And he walked away down the road, chewing on the books as he went.

The Witch was back at the bus stop. She'd found her little dog and was busy tying a pink ribbon onto its head to make it more attractive to children.

'Did you find the library, boy?' she asked.

'Yes.'

'Yes *what?*'

'Uhhhh... Yes, I did.'

'You're a very impolite little boy!'

'Thank you.'

THWACK!

'Ow. Now I need a chocolate shop.'

'Now I need a chocolate shop, *please.*'

'Oh, do you? So do I - shall we go together?'

'You idiot boy! (*Thwack!*) Rover! Bite his toes off! Rover! *Come back here!* Rover, *bite*! No! Not *my* toes, *his* toes! Owwwww!'

Finally the Thundertroll found a chocolate shop, and knocked on the door....

Crash... splinter... tinkle...

The troll said to himself, 'I must remember that – trolls should not knock on glass doors.'

The shop assistant looked up from the counter as the Thundertroll walked in.

'What would you like?' he asked.

'A bigggg box of chocolates!'

'Pooh! Your breath is like a stinkbomb! What *have* you been eating?'

'A children's book about dark materials. It wasn't very good...'

'It must have been rotten. What *you* need now is mouthwash!'

'Have you got chocolate mouthwash?'

'No!'

'I want a biggggg -'

'We don't have those, either! Chocolate bunnies, Santas, eggs and even mice, but NO chocolate pigs.'

'I don't want a pig. I just want a box of chocolates. A biggggg -'

'All right, all right! There's plenty of boxes on the shelves.'

'Can I take any one I like?'

'Yes, of course.'

'Good... I'll have this one then - bye!' And the Thundertroll started out through the door with an enormous box of chocolates, almost as big as himself.

'No! Come back here, you STUPID boy!'

The Thundertroll walked back inside, puzzled. He said, 'Yes... what do you want?'

'You have to pay for the chocolates first.'

'Why?'

'Because - because - because you have to, that's all!'

The Thundertroll thought for a while. Then he said, 'Uh... I haven't got any library tickets.... I ate them.'

'You don't pay for chocolates with library tickets! You *must* know that!'

'Must I? I'll try to remember it, then.' The Thunder-troll thought hard as he repeated the shop assistant's words. 'You don't pay for chocolates with library tickets... Right, I got that now - bye!' He headed for the door again.

'No! Come back here!'

'Yes...? What do you want this time?'

'Look, you stupid troglodyte, you have to pay with *money*.'

'Oh. Mummy never gave me any money... what is it?'

'It's *this* – look!' The shop assistant opened the cash till. '*This* is money.'

The Thundertroll reached his hand into the till and took out a great wad of banknotes. 'I got plenty of money now!' he shouted.

'PUT IT BACK!!'

The shop manager heard the shouting and came hurrying out of a back room.

'What's the trouble, Mr Prendergast?' he asked. 'Can't you manage a simple sale? What does the ugly little child want?'

'He wants a box of chocolates, Sir.'

'So what's the problem? Everyone who comes in here wants chocolate. We're a *chocolate* shop, Mr Prendergast!'

'But he hasn't any money!'

'I got plenty of money!' exclaimed the Thundertroll, waving the banknotes.

The manager said, 'He has plenty of money, Mr Prendergast, so sell him a box of chocolates. He can't help being that horrible colour.'

'But - but –'

The Thundertroll gave all the money to the shop assistant and left the shop with his box of chocolates.

The Thundertroll walked along road, looking for the place where the next lightning bolt would strike. He said to himself, 'It ought to come down just about HERE.'

As it happened, the Witch was passing by with her dog - *and* a bulging shopping bag. She asked, 'The bus is going to stop just about here, did you say?'

'Not a bus, a bolt of lightning!'

'No, there's nothing *frightening* about a bus. I've been travelling on them for years! I know, I'll wait here with you. I need to get home quickly and put something in the oven.' She looked down at her shopping bag, and smiled.

'Look, lady - this isn't a safe place to be. You've gotta go to the other side.'

'Oh, the bus queue is on the other side of you? Well, I don't see why *I* should move. When I was young, we always let our elders get on the bus first.'

'No – listen: A BIG LIGHTNING BOLT IS GOING TO COME DOWN OUT OF THE SKY!'

'Ohhhh... the bus is going to come down out of the sky, is it? Isn't science marvellous? In my day, they just used to drive along the road.'

'You stupid human...'

'What did you call me?' (*Thwack!* went the big umbrella)

'Just move aside - it's coming now!'

'The bus is coming, is it? I'll put my arm up to tell it to stop...'

A lightning bolt came whizzing down out of the sky and struck the Witch, who fell and knocked over her shopping bag, so that everything spilled out of it… and escaped.

'Ow! He bit me!' she cried. 'Just like my dog…'

The Spell

The littlest Thundertroll grabbed the lightning bolt and slid up it all the way home, his big box of choco-lates tucked under one arm.

He hurried back to the cloud apartment where the Thundertroll Fairy lived, and knocked on the door.

'Go away!' growled the Fairy from inside.

The littlest Thundertroll kicked the door down again and went in.

This time the Thundertroll Fairy was sitting in a bath in the middle of the floor, eating toffee popcorn, drinking ginger beer and watching Fairy Wrestling on television.

'Waddya want this time?' he growled.

'Please, Thundertroll Fairy, I brought you that box of chocolates you asked for.'

'Oh, yeah.' The Thundertroll Fairy got out of the bath and pulled out the plug so that the bath water ran out onto the carpet. Then he waded over to the window and dried himself on the curtains.

'Let's have it then, Shorty.'

He took the huge box of chocolates from the Thundertroll and slotted the whole box into his mouth, without even taking the wrapping off. It fitted rather snugly and he had to shove it in.

Mnrfhhh grnnnnph hrrrmpshhhhh.....

And he swallowed it whole.

'Burp! Thanks, little Trog. Now push off.'

'No - you promised! You said you would do a spell for me so I can throw lightning bolts that go zing zang KAPOWIE!'

'Oh yeah, right... Okay. Now, where's my wand?'

You'll know of course that an ordinary fairy has a sweet little wand with a twinkly star on the end. Not the Thundertroll Fairy. *He* went to the fridge and got out a sausage.

He waved the sausage at the littlest Thundertroll and recited a spell: *'Wongy, dongy, bongy pongy. Whizz pizz slurmspringle. Whoosh Whoosh Whoosh!'*

The sausage went all floppy.

'Oh dear - it didn't work. See, the end's gone green. Must have gone off when I used it to write a letter to my Mummy.'

He flung the sausage out of the window. It fell all the way down to Human-land, where it landed behind a bus shelter and was eaten by a dog hiding there, named Rover. Rover was immediately transformed into Wonder Dog and flew away to do mighty deeds, never to be a Witch's dog again…

The Thundertroll Fairy went back to the fridge and got another sausage.

'This is a premium pork sausage from Sainsbury's. They always work. Uh, I'll try a different spell, too. Let's see – Slurzy wongle pongy doodle, wozzledingy bumdiddle! Whang! Dongy! Pow!'

The sausage made a sizzling sound.

'Yeah, that one worked - look, you can tell cos' it's cooked. Your lightning bolts will work better now…'

'Thank you, Thundertroll Fairy!'

'My pleasure. Hey! – That's unusual… Look, the spell also turned my left foot into a hedgehog! Here hedgehog, have a bite of sausage…'

The Lightning Bolt Jamboree

As it happened, there was just a week left before the big annual Lightning Bolt Jamboree. The littlest Thundertroll spent every day making new lightning bolts, testing them, sharpening them, testing them again, bending them to a new shape, and so on.

When the day of the Jamboree came, once again he was standing between his father and the King of all the Thundertrolls. The King leaned down and patted him on the head again. *Hard.*

'HOW ARE YOU, MY CHILD? VERY NICE TO SEE YOU AGAIN! HAR HAR HAR! HO HO HO!'

(Pat Pat Pat!)

'Ow! Stupid old man...'

The littlest Thundertroll threw his first bolt.

Zip .... zap

zip....   zap...

zppppst...

'Ohhhhh... it didn't work! I can't have thrown it hard enough....'

He tried the next one.

'This is better...'

Zing...   Zing...!

'Hey - where's it going?'

Zing... Zoing...

Zoing...!

'It's coming back!'

Zoong... Zoong... **Zoong**...!

'Oh no! It's going to hit me in the - !'

And it hit him right in…

… the posterior.

'Owwwwwwwww!'

The King had watched all this and was very amused. He roared:

'THAT'S VERY FUNNY! HARR HARR HO HO HO!'
(*Pat Pat Pat!*)

The littlest Thundertroll threw his next bolt, even harder this time.

Zing... Zing... ZING!

'Hey - where's it going **this** time?'

Zing... Zoing... ZOING...!

'It's coming back again!'

Zoong...   Zoong...
ZOOONG...!

'Oh no! It's going to –'

And it hit the King of the Thundertrolls right in...

...the posterior.

'OOOOOOOOHHH...!'

The littlest Thundertroll thought it would only be fair if he patted the King on the head the way the King patted *him*. So he climbed up the back of the King's trousers and then up his shirt, onto his shoulder, onto his head; and then he jumped up and down on the King's head, shouting,

'Very funny! Har Har Har! Ho Ho Ho!'

The King said to himself, 'WHAT'S THAT ON MY HEAD? A FLY?'

Whack!

'Owwwww!'

The littlest Thundertroll looked around. This was a good place to throw his last two lightning bolts from. He took out the first one, bent it, felt the point, and said to it, 'Come on, baby!'

He gave it a kiss.

⚡ *!ZAP!* ⚡

'Owwww... I must remember – I must not kiss lightning bolts...'

He stepped back and threw the bolt with all his might.

ZZZZZZIIINGGGG!

But he'd thrown it downwards too much. It went through the top of the King's head and the tip of it popped out of the bottom of his chin.

The littlest Thundertroll heard a muffled kingly voice saying, 'OOOOH - what's this, then?' The King pulled the bolt out of his chin and peered at it.

'A LITLE LIGHTNING BOLT?!!'

He flung it down and it whizzed all the way to the ground and exploded in a bus stop by the foot of what looked like an old lady with a large shopping bag.

('Ouch! Does that mean there's a bus coming?')

The littlest Thundertroll had only one bolt left. He took it out of his lightning bolt holder, tested the point, and tested its bendiness. 'Come on, baby!' he said. But this time he remembered not to kiss it.

He threw it harder than he'd ever thrown anything.

ZIPPPPP!   ZIIIIING!
ZZZZZZOOOING!

('It's doing it!')

ZZZZZZZONNNNNGGG!

ZOOOING!

('It's gonna make it!')

ZIIIII -

But the lightning bolt stopped in mid-air, just two

metres above the ground.

'Oh, BOTHER!!' exclaimed the Thundertroll.

But he wasn't going to give up now. He tied the top of the lightning bolt to the King's hair and slid down the bolt.

He fell off the end…

… and landed in a bus shelter.

'Is that you, Rover?' asked a familiar voice. 'Is that my little doggie come back to me?'

'No, it's me.'

Now, the Thundertroll had a problem. He was only a metre tall, and the tip of the lightning bolt was another metre above his head.

The Witch said, 'I know you! You're that rude little boy I met the other day. Can I help you?'

'No! Stay where you are!'

'That's the problem with the young people of today, they won't accept help from us older people who know better than they do!'

'I don't need any help!'

'Yes you do. I know, why don't you have a look in my new, extra-strong shopping bag. I think I have some sweeties in there…'

'I don't want any sweeties. I just (*jump*) need (*jump*) to reach that (*jump*) thing up there.'

'You mean that shiny thing? Here, let me do it…'

'No!'

'I insist! I'm not useless, you know!'

⚡ ⚡ ⚡POW!!!!!!!!!!!! ⚡ ⚡ ⚡

'Oh… He bit me again - just like my dog!'

Endings

✗ It was a bad ending for the Witch, because being struck by lightning so many times completely ruined her appetite for children, so she had to eat fish and chips instead. And she *hated* fish and chips.

✗ But it was a good ending for the Thundertroll Fairy, because he could watch goblin wrestling on TV without having his door kicked down.

✗ Finally, it was a good ending for the littlest Thundertroll, because he had finally got one of his lightning bolts to reach the ground…

… and after that, his lightning bolts *always* worked.

The Princess and the Golden Ball

The voices

The **Princess** has one of those lazy, smug, self-satisfied voices used in TV advertisements for beauty products. But when she doesn't get her own way, she sulks and her voice changes to a nasty whine. When she grows up, she wants to be a pop star with no talent.

Her Mother the Queen is the most brainless woman imaginable. She says foolish things in an upper class accent so polished that you could shine the silver with it. She has problems with words of more than five letters, but since her words are pronounced so perfectly, she imagines she must always be saying something frightfully clever.

The **King** is... well, the King. He's in charge of *everything* (except for his daughter) and expects people to jump when he says "Ju-". His voice is rich and deep and confident, and you just know from the sound of it that you'd better not argue with him, unless you want to be slightly shorter.

The **Head Goldsmith** sounds worried. As he should be.

The **Old Man** has a mild and thoughtful voice, to match his mild and thoughtful manner. He speaks in an unrushed, courteous way, and is probably an ancient Professor of Magical Studies at some hidden school.

The **Frog** is totally chilled. You can tell from his voice that he's an amusing guy who likes to party a lot, and then sleep a lot – at the bottom of a pond, maybe, but hey, that's cool, you know? He's not sure he can be bothered with all this golden ball stuff, but he'll give it a whirl.

The story

Once upon a time, there was a princess…

A selfish, spoiled, bad-tempered, evil-natured, pig-greedy and bone idle princess.

One morning, the Princess looked up from her breakfast cereal and announced, 'I want another birthday present!'

The King said, 'Of course, my precious!'

The Queen looked puzzled. 'But your birthday was last month, wasn't it?' she asked. 'I'm sure you had plenty of presents then.'

The Princess took out a little diary. 'I have had exactly 143 presents,' she said. 'But I want one more. I deserve it! *I'm worth it!*'

'Of course you deserve it, Princess,' said the King. 'You're so *very* special!'

'I want exactly 144 presents this year,' insisted the Princess. 'That makes one of those special numbers, doesn't it, Daddy?'

The King counted very slowly on his fingers. '144 is twelve times twelve,' he said a few minutes later. 'Since you're twelve yourself, it's a very good number of presents to receive.'

'144 is also called *one gross,* isn't it?' said her mother helpfully. 'Doesn't that mean something good?' (The Queen was even less intelligent than the rest of the family). 'A *gross* of presents for my *gross* girl! What would you like, my darling?'

The Princess said, 'I want a ball made out of gold, as big as my hands but as light as a feather. Like a big, golden balloon.'

'Oh,' said her father. 'That would be very hard to make…'

The Princess howled, 'You don't love me! You *never* loved me!'

The King wrung his hands and said frantically, 'My dear, dear Princess, my poppet! I didn't mean it was *impossible*. Just *very difficult*! I'll get the royal goldsmiths started on it immediately.'

'Really?' The Princess was suddenly all smiles.

'Of course! After all, you're –'

'I know,' said the Princess with a self-satisfied sigh. 'I'm worth it.'

A few days later, the Head Goldsmith came to the palace and knelt before the King and Princess. 'It's not possible to make a golden ball as light as a feather,' he said. 'I've tried.'

The Princess shouted, 'Off with his head!'

'Or maybe it *is* possible,' the Head Goldsmith quickly changed his mind, 'but it's going to take a long time. Several months, probably.'

'I *won't* wait that long!' the Princess shouted. 'Daddy, have his head cut off *now*!'

The King said, 'But if I have his head cut off, who's going to make you a golden ball, my precious?'

'I don't care!'

And so the poor Head Goldsmith had his head cut off. As did the Deputy Head Goldsmith, when he too failed to make a golden ball as light as a feather. And one by one, all the goldsmiths turned up with golden balls not big enough or not light enough to satisfy the Princess.

They ran out of goldsmiths, and tried the magicians. The Grand Master Magician couldn't do it.

Chop!

The Master Magician couldn't, either.

Chop!

And their two magical apprentices couldn't even *spell* "gold".

Chop! Chop!

An Odd Visitor

Next, the King placed an advertisement in the Kingdom's newspaper, *The Chopping Block*. It read:

~~Golden ball required~~
Must be light as a feather
Must be at least two Royal handwidths wide
Bring to the Palace at 9 am, any day of the week
Royal reward awaits successful applicant
Nasty end awaits all others

Not surprisingly, no one came… until one day, an old man with a grey beard down to his knees was shown into the throne room. He bowed to the King, the Queen and the Princess.

'There's just one problem,' said the old man. 'There's only one magician in the world who's good enough to make such a ball, and he might not want to do it. You would have to ask him nicely.'

The King was deeply shocked 'Ask him?' he exclaimed. '*Ask* him? **ASK** him?!! I'm the King! I don't *ASK* for *anything*! I will **ORDER** him to do it!'

The Princess added, 'And if he *doesn't* do it, we'll have his head chopped off! That's right, isn't it, Daddy?'

'That's right, my Princess. We Royals expect full obedience. None of this *asking* nonsense.'

'Yes,' said the Princess. 'Because we're worth it.'

The old man bowed his head again. He said with a sigh, 'Unfortunately, that attitude might get you into all sorts of trouble. Don't say I didn't warn you.'

'Off with his – !' began the Princess.

But it was too late. The old man's head had already gone - disappeared with the rest of him, in a puff of green smoke.

A day later, the same old man returned, carrying something in a bag.

'I myself am the great magician I told you about,' he said quietly. 'I am prepared to fulfil your unusual request, but -'

'It's *not* a request,' interrupted the King rudely. 'It's a command!'

'It's a *double* command!' exclaimed the Princess. '*He* commands you and *I* command you!'

'It's a *triple* command!' said the Queen, 'because *I* command you, too. Wait - it's more than that! It's for the Princess' 144th present, so it's a *gross* command!' She clapped her hands at her own cleverness.

The Magician said, 'Yes, your Majesty. I'm sure it *is* a gross command –'

'For my gross Princess!'

'No doubt that is true as well,' he agreed. 'Now, in this bag I have a magical golden ball. But the great magic it contains must be used properly. It –'

'Give it to me!' the Princess shouted, running up and pulling at the bag.

'What's the little word with the big meaning?' asked the Magician.

'That's easy,' said the Princess. 'Give – it – to – me – NOW!'

'I'll give you a clue,' said the Magician, hiding the bag behind his back. 'It starts with the letter "p".'

'Guards!' shouted the Princess. 'Seize this old man! Take the bag off him! Beat him! Whip him! Boil him in oil! Chop off his head!'

And she said a lot of other words, none of them beginning with the letter "p". Except for one:

'Prison!' she shouted to the guards, who grabbed the old man and started dragging him away.

'A final word of advice,' said the Magician. 'Don't take the ball anywhere near water.'

'I never take advice,' said the Princess.

'That's true,' added the King. 'She's most wondrously independent.'

'*Grossly* independent,' said the Queen helpfully.

'I thought as much,' said the Magician. And he gave a little bow, then disappeared again in a puff of smoke – red smoke this time.

The Pond

The Princess took the golden ball out into the royal garden and played with it happily for hours.

It was certainly magical, for when she threw it into the air, it would hover there, spinning and making a wonderful humming sound before falling gently back into her hands.

And when she held it to her ear – ah! It seemed to be singing softly and rather sadly, in beautiful words she couldn't quite understand.

But then she came to the royal pond. She immediately recalled the old man's advice and was very, very angry.

'I'm a Princess!' she exclaimed. 'I will *not* be told what to do! I *will* be obeyed!' Then she smiled sweetly at her reflection in the pond and added:

'Because I'm worth it!'

She threw the ball into the water, commanding it to float. And indeed it should have floated, for it was larger than a tennis ball and much lighter.

But mysteriously, the ball sank like a stone and came to rest next to a big, ugly, wart-covered frog.

The ball lay there at the bottom of pond, glimmering and gleaming and glistening up at the Princess, who stamped her feet and raged at the ball, the frog, the old man and the whole universe.

The frog opened its eyes, yawned, stretched its long, green, warty legs and launched itself upwards. When it reached the surface of the pond, it swam towards the Princess.

Oddly, it swam on its back.

It hopped onto a rock and yawned again. It had the longest, reddest tongue you can imagine and the brightest, blackest froggy eyes you've ever seen, and the coldest, slimiest skin you've ever touched.

'I suppose you'll be wanting the ball back?' it asked lazily.

'Get me the ball,' the Princess ordered.

The frog shook its head disapprovingly. 'What's the little word with the big meaning?' it asked.

'Not you as well!' the Princess said, stamping her feet some more.

'Too many words. And all of them wrong,' said the frog. 'Look, I'll give you a clue, bossy boots. It's what you say when you want something.'

'That's easy,' said the Princess. 'Get me the ball, OR ELSE!'

'Nah. That's not it, either. Try the *polite* way of asking for something. It begins with the letter –'

'I KNOW!' the Princess shouted. 'You want me to say the "p" word. Well, you can give up *that* idea. I'm an Important Person. Important People don't have to use words like that.'

'In that case,' said the frog, 'I'll keep the ball until you've learned some new words.' And it hopped back into the pond, swam to the bottom and curled up next to the golden ball for a nap.

The Princess stamped around the pond some more. She fumed and stewed and hissed and steamed and finally boiled over. She said several words, none of them beginning with the letter "p". Then she shouted one word very loud:

'GUARDS!'

The guards came running up. She pointed at the pond.

'Drain it!' she commanded. 'You'll find a golden ball at the bottom, and a large, ugly frog. Squash the frog flat, cut off his legs, make him into a frog kebab, cook him on the royal barbecue, and feed him to the royal wolfhounds. And bring the golden ball to me.'

She paused dramatically. There were some little words with big meanings which needed to be said. She said them now:

'Do it *now*, and do it *right*. Or else the royal barbecue will have some *bigger* kebabs.'

An hour later, a trembling guard came to report.

'Your Highness, we drained the pond. Nothing. No frog, no ball. We even dug up all the mud from the bottom. I'm very sorry.'

He closed his eyes, waiting for the Princess to say those four little words: *Off with his head.*

But the Princess was so angry that she stormed away immediately, quite forgetting to make any arrangements for guard-sized kebabs on the royal barbecue. She went and threw herself onto her bed and sulked there all evening.

She was still sulking when the Royal Storyteller came in and asked, 'What story would the dear Princess want to hear tonight?'

The Princess hissed, 'I want a story about a frog which dies a horrible death!'

The Royal Storyteller was puzzled. She said, 'The only stories I know about frogs are ones where they turn out to be enchanted princes. But I can make up a new one, I suppose. Once upon a time –'

'Stop!' shouted the Princess. 'That's it! Of course!'

Excitedly she told the Royal Storyteller all about the frog and the golden ball. And the Royal Storyteller agreed that the frog MUST be something very special indeed.

The Royal Storyteller exclaimed, 'He swims on his back! He talks! And then he mysteriously disappears! He *must* be enchanted!'

The Princess smiled. Not a nice smile. A crafty, greedy, selfish, lying little smile. A *gross* smile.

'So,' she said, smiling her gross smile again, 'all I have to do is find the frog and then do whatever he asks. Afterwards, he'll turn into a handsome prince and marry me. I'll be rich beyond even *my* wildest dreams, and he'll spoil me even more than I'm being spoiled already. *And* I'll get the ball back! All I have to do is fool a stupid frog…'

Fooling the Frog

The Princess ordered the pond to be refilled overnight. And early the next morning, she went to the pond all alone. She was wearing her silkiest, prettiest royal robes. She'd had her hair curled and her nails painted and her lips sticked. A darling little tear was trembling at the corner of each eye.

She leaned close to the water. 'Froggy!' she whispered. '*Dear* froggy! Oh, *lovely* froggy, do come and speak to me. I'm so, so sorry…'

Just as she'd hoped, the frog rose to the surface of

the water. 'What do you want this time?' it asked grumpily. 'I was just having a lovely dream and you've spoiled it.'

'Oh, froggy, I'm so sorry! It's just that – that –' and the Princess burst into tears.

(I must say in her defence that these were real tears. You see, she really was sad: sad that she'd lost the ball, and sad that she'd messed up her first chance to snag a really good special-offer fairy-tale prince…

… And the other reason they were real tears was that in the lacy handkerchief she was pressing to her eyes, she had hidden an onion.)

'All right, all right,' said the frog crossly. 'Enough of the crying, already. What do you want?'

'Can I have my ball back –' here the Princess drew a deep breath, crossed her fingers behind her back, and said a word she'd never used before, '- please?'

The frog thought about this. 'If you want your ball back, you'll have to take me into your room,' he said.

(Good, thought the Princess, *that's just what fairy tale frog princes always ask for.)*

'And you'll have to let me eat from your plate.'

'That would be lovely,' she lied.

'And let me sleep on a pillow next to your bed.'

'There's nothing I would like more,' she lied again.

'And kiss me goodnight.'

'Why, of course!'

'And tell me a story.'

'I think I can manage that.'

'Say my prayers with me.'

'Well, I suppose so…'

'Sing me a lullaby, too.'

'If you insist.'

'And stroke my cold, slimy, warty little head until I fall asleep.'

Oh yuk, yuk, yukky-doo! the Princess said to herself. But aloud she promised, 'Certainly I will!'

The frog dived into the pond and returned with the golden ball. The Princess looked at him with tears in her eyes (she'd been at the onion again) and said,

'You can come for supper at 7 pm.'

The frog looked at her doubtfully. 'Just one thing about this dinner,' he said. 'No kebabs.'

The Magic Works!

The Princess kept her promises. The frog had a lovely dinner, was told a wondrous story, had his prayers listened to (the Princess didn't join in) and then was lifted onto a soft, soft pillow.

The Princess kissed him once on his cold, slimy head and quickly turned her head away, wiped her lips and muttered several words which didn't begin with the letter "p".

Then the frog settled down to sleep while the Princess stroked his slippery, warty skin and sang him a royal lullaby.

'By the way,' he murmured as he was dropping off, 'I'm probably an enchanted prince, you know.'

'Oh, really?' she asked in a surprised sort of way. 'I hadn't thought of that.'

'You wouldn't be doing all this just to get my gold and silver and jewels, would you?' he asked sleepily.

'What, me? Of course not!'

'You wouldn't be pretending to be kind and loving and generous because you think I'll turn out to be a handsome prince, and marry you?'

'Never!' cried the Princess. But she had her fingers firmly crossed behind her back again. You see, she had this silly idea that lies don't count if you cross your fingers when you tell them.

What she didn't know is that this just turns the lies into *gross* lies, and makes them count double: once for the lying, and once for trying to hide it.

... And when she awoke in the morning, there on the floor by her bed, sound asleep, was the most gorgeous, manly-looking prince she could have imagined. And to judge by his golden, bejewelled crown and his golden armbands and his big golden belt buckle, he was enormously rich, too.

She crept to the edge of the bed and gazed down at him greedily. *I did it!* she thought. *I fooled him and now he's mine, all mine! Him and the golden ball and riches beyond counting! Oh, I'm REALLY worth it now!*

But just then an odd thing happened to her. There was a pesky fly buzzing about the room, and it landed on the pillow next to her. And suddenly, without a thought, she stuck out her tongue at it.

Which was a very rude thing to do.

And her tongue shot out an awfully long way, hit the fly, and then snapped back into her mouth, with the fly all wrapped up inside it.
Oh yuk!

Oh double yuk!

Oh yuk 144 times! **GROSS** *yuk!*

She had a sudden, terrible thought. She hopped to the end of her bed and looked at herself in the large mirror hanging on the wall opposite.

It was as she suspected: the frog had turned into a handsome prince, but she –

She had turned into a frog.

A fat, ugly frog with slimy green skin spotted with dark warts. With a wide mouth and a long, red sticky tongue. With those horrid, crooked froggy legs front and back. She glared at herself in the mirror. '*Gross!*' she croaked.

And what about the golden ball? The Princess looked to where she had put the ball on the floor, on the other side of the bed.

The ball really had been magical, she could tell that now: for it had turned into a lovely, lovely princess with love and kindness and generosity written in her beautiful face.

The Princess couldn't bear to watch anyone else being happy, so she hopped out of the room and then down the white marble front steps of the palace. She was joined there by two larger frogs.

And as the frog princess and her green, warty parents hopped away towards the pond, they croaked to themselves several words…

… none of them beginning with the letter "p".

Snow White
and the Seven Easter Bunnies

The voices

The **Wicked Queen's** voice is so icy cold that you could skate on it. She's beautiful, and she knows it. She's rich and knows it, too. She's evil and *everyone* knows it. But her voice isn't evil: it's beautiful and rich and musical. However, it's also as cold as winter, as if she would happily chop you up and put you in a pie. Which of course is true.

Snow White is young and sweet and innocent and not the brightest of princesses (if she was, she'd be called Snow Bright instead). Her voice is clear and kind and she always sounds a little surprised by life, because she always is.

The **Magic Mirror** is wonderfully refined and sounds like an old-style BBC Radio announcer. He's the sort of ex-prince who calls everyone "darling" and speaks of having a "stupendous time" at the Ball. He pronounces every word perfectly.

The **Bunnies** are a tough bunch of desperados. They talk like cops from Hill Street Blues, Miami Vice and CSI. Imagine a policeman in a bunny suit bursting into the room and shouting, 'Drop that carrot! And back away from it reaaaaal slow!'

The **Soldiers** talk like all those other mindless persons who do or say dreadful things and then just shrug their shoulders afterwards, as if it doesn't matter. They congratulate themselves on always doing a good job, which in their case is killing things without asking too many questions.

The story

Scene 1 Background

Long ago, back when there were no cars, no clocks, no telephones and no Krispy Kreme doughnuts, in the fairy tale kingdom called Pastiche there was a King whose wife had died, leaving him with a 15 year old daughter named Snow White.

There was also a young lady who was very, very beautiful and very, very wicked. This beautiful and wicked lady accidentally on purpose met the King at a dance. She danced both beautifully and wickedly, and soon the poor king fell in love with her dancing and with her beauty (he didn't know about her wickedness).

So he married her, and then accidentally on purpose he died... by which I mean he met with a nasty accident, but it happened totally on purpose – the Queen's purpose.

Snow White was now 16. She was good and kind, and had a lovely smile. The beautiful and wicked Queen was only ten years older than Snow White, so she had a choice of treating Snow White like a daughter, or a sister.

But she was wicked woman, so she decided to treat her …

… like a slug instead.

Scene 2 The Sorting of the Princes

The Queen was bored, and was looking for someone to take the place of the old king. So she advertised in the newspapers of nearby kingdoms for princes who were brave, rich, handsome, had all their own teeth, didn't mind being told what to do, and could count up to 10.

In time, 60 princes turned up. They took their counting exams (half of them failed), had their teeth checked (two failed), had their bravery checked by being put into cages with fierce lions (10 of them cried and were sent home, another 5 didn't cry but did get eaten), and had their handsomeness measured by a panel of lady judges (5 were rejected and were sent back to see the lions again).

There were eight princes remaining. The final test was on Easter Day – though as it happens, Easter hadn't been invented yet.

They were all sent in together to see the Queen. She turned to the first and asked sweetly:

'What kind of women do you most like looking at?'

The prince said honestly, 'Slim, blonde women.'

'Wrong!' she cried. She waved a wand… there was a flash of light… and he turned into a bunny (number 1).

She asked the next prince the same question. He looked at the Queen, who was tall and dark-haired, and lied, 'Tall women with dark hair.'

'Wrong!' she cried. She waved a wand… another flash… and he too turned into a bunny (2).

The next said nervously, '*Very* tall and *very* dark?'

'Wrong!' *Zap, ping, pow*… hop hop hop (3).

'*Rather* tall and with long, er, sort of darkish hair?'

'Wrong!' *Zap, ping, pow* … hop hop hop (4).

'Ummm… I – uh -'

'Too late!' *Zap, ping, pow* … hop hop hop (5).

'Magnificent, queenly women with a superb wand technique?'

'Good try, but still wrong!' *Zap, ping, pow* … hop hop hop (6).

The seventh prince wasn't very bright (he'd actually cheated on the counting test by writing the numbers on his fingers). He said, 'I like lookin' at short, fat women with no hair at all.'

'Wrong!' *Zap, ping, pow* … hop hop hop (7).

One prince was left, and he was sweating by now. But he flashed a confident princey-type smile and said, 'The only woman I like looking at is *YOU*.'

'Right!' The Queen smiled beautifully and raised her wand.

The prince's smile wavered. 'Ah, but my lovely Queen,' he said, 'if I answered the question correctly, why are you pointing that dangerous wand at me?'

'Simple,' said the Queen. '*You* only want to look at *me*. And I'm going to make your dreams come true!' She pointed the wand and – *Zap, ping, pow!* …

… The 8th prince turned into a magic mirror, which the royal mirror-fastener put on the wall of the Queen's special mirror room, which was full of mirrors (though this was the only magic one).

And the 7 Easter Bunnies hopped away as quietly as possible, because they didn't want to be taken to visit the lions again.

Scene 3 The Magic Mirror

The Queen stood before her magic mirror and commanded:
  'Mirror, mirror on the wall,
  Who's the fairest of them all?'

The mirror replied:
  'SNOW WHITE IS ALWAYS FAIR AND TRUE
  BUT *YOU* CHEAT AT EVERYTHING YOU DO!'

'Thank you,' said the Queen. 'I'm pleased that you

noticed. But I wasn't talking about fair *behaviour*. I was talking about *beauty*. Who's the most beautiful woman in the kingdom?'

'THAT'S EASY. IT'S YOU, YOU, YOU!'

'Right answer!'

The mirror said, 'SNOW WHITE LOOKS A LITTLE ORDINARY COMPARED WITH YOU.'

'*How* ordinary?' the Queen asked in a dangerous voice, with her wand poised in the air.

'OH, **VERY** ORDINARY,' the mirror said quickly.

'Maybe even a little bit ugly?'

'OH YES, YES, WITHOUT A DOUBT.'

'Would you say she looks like the back end of a bus, maybe?'

'NO, MY QUEEN.'

'Why not?'

'BECAUSE BUSES HAVEN'T BEEN INVENTED YET.'

Every day the Queen asked questions like:

'Who's the prettiest?'

'YOU.'

'The most famous?'

'YOU, WITHOUT A DOUBT!'

'The nicest?'

'SNOW WHITE.'

'That's okay. I HATE nice people. And the richest?'

'YOURSELF, QUEENIE-BABES.'

'*Queenie-babes*? Watch your tongue, or I'll turn you off like a bad TV program!'

'TV HASN'T BEEN INVENTED YET.'

'Then watch your step, mirror!'

'MIRRORS DON'T HAVE STEPS. IF WE DID, WE WOULDN'T BE MIRRORS, WE'D BE STAIRCASES.'

… And one day she asked suspiciously, '… Who's

the *second* fairest?'

The mirror said: 'THE SECOND FAIREST IS ANDROMEDA SNOZ-ZLEBUCKET OF GLOBWATER, AND SHE'S REALLY CUTE.'

The Queen went pink with anger and shouted, 'Then I'll take care of *her*! Ha Ha! Hee Hee! Ho Ho!'

The Queen shouted to her servants to get her carriage, and they drove to Globwater with her shouting all the way, "Faster! Faster!".

She went straight to the home of poor Andromeda Snozzlebucket, waved her wand, laughed twice, and drove back to the castle in a much better mood.

And poor Andromeda found her pretty face disfigured by an enormous wart. I mean, ENORMOUS.

And every few weeks the Wicked Queen would hurry to the house of yet another lady who was almost as pretty as herself and cast an uglifying spell:

- ✕ Some she gave big noses.
    - ✕ Others, noses as tiny as a button.
        - ✕ And some received noses with big moles on the end that glowed in the dark.
- ✕ For some, she took their hair away.
    - ✕ For others, she made their hair grow even more… including a fine moustache!
- ✕ Some she gave squint eyes.
    - ✕ Some she gave an extra eye, which was actually quite useful if you wanted to see what was going on behind you.

… And all because she wanted to make sure that she was still the fairest of them all.

But about a year later, it happened....

'Magic Mirror on the wall...'
'YOU'RE STILL NUMBER 1, QUEEN OF MY DREAMS. BUT LITTLE SNOW WHITE IS CATCHING UP FAST!'

'What? *That* ugly brat? I'll take care of *her*! I'll make her left ear twice the size of the right one! Ha Ha! Hee Hee! Ho Ho!'

And the Magic Mirror said:

> 'THERE WAS AN OLD MAN OF DEVIZES
> WHO HAD EARS OF DIFFERENT SIZES.
> THE ONE THAT WAS SMALL WAS OF NO USE AT ALL
> BUT THE OTHER WON SEVERAL PRIZES!'

The Queen asked, 'What was *that*?'
'THAT WAS A LIMERICK, AS WRITTEN BY A MAN CALLED EDWARD LEAR IN ENGLAND. IT'S A KIND OF RHYMING POEM THAT.... HASN'T BEEN INVENTED YET.'

Anyway, the Queen went into Snow White's room, waved her wand once, laughed twice, and went out again in a much better mood.

Snow White didn't mind. She dyed the big ear green and dyed the small ear blue, put glitter on them both, put a big earring on the small ear and a small earring on the big ear... and went back to what she liked doing most, which was singing, visiting with her friends, and going to school – even though school hadn't been invented yet.

... And a month or so afterwards:

The Wicked Queen asked, 'Magic Mirror on the wall... '
'SNOW WHITE.'
'What?! How?'
'SNOW WHITE HAS STARTED A NEW FASHION. EVERYONE WANTS THEIR EARS TO BE DIFFERENT SIZES AND DIFFERENT COLOURS NOW.'

'That *devious* child! I know - I'll take away her hair! Ha Ha! Hee Hee! Ho Ho!'
'*THAT* SHOULD TEACH HER A LESSON...'

So the Queen went into Snow White's room again, waved her wand once, laughed twice, and went out again in a much better mood.

Snow White didn't mind. She made herself wonderful wigs out of the oddest things –

bits of coloured string

flowers

book covers (even though books hadn't been invented yet)

spaghetti

and those long sugary sour sweets that look like worms...

A few weeks later:

'Magic Mirror on the –'

'SNOW WHITE. EVERY OTHER WOMAN IN THE KINGDOM HAS CUT OFF HER HAIR AND IS FOLLOWING THE NEW SNOW WHITE NO-HAIR FASHION. HER FACE AND HER HAIR ARE ON EVERY WOMAN'S MAGAZINE.'

'But –'

'AH YES. SORRY, I FORGOT. WOMEN'S MAGAZINES HAVEN'T BEEN INVENTED YET...'

'I'll just make her look *ordinary*, then! Normal ears, normal hair, but ugly. Like the back end of a... of something that hasn't been invented yet. Ha Ha! Hee Hee! Ho Ho!'

This time it worked. And the Evil Queen might have stopped there, but she got bored with just being the prettiest, richest and most fashionable woman in the world. She started asking the mirror more difficult questions, such as:

'Who's the *happiest* one of all?'

'OH, THAT WOULD BE SNOW WHITE FOR CERTAIN.'

'What? I'm the richest, and prettiest and – and all that stuff – how can *she* be happier than *me*? It's not right! It's not *fair*!'

'THAT IS TRUE, MY QUEEN. BUT SHE'S HAPPY AT HOME, SHE'S HAPPY WITH HER FRIENDS, AND SHE'S HAPPY AT SCHOOL, DESPITE THE FACT THAT SCHOOL HASN'T BEEN INVENTED YET. SHE HAS AN EVIL QUEEN FOR A STEPMOTHER, BUT EVEN THAT DOESN'T BOTHER HER.'

'I'll take care of *that*! I'll put her in prison! Ha Ha! Hee Hee! Ho Ho!'

'*THAT* SHOULD TEACH HER A LESSON...'

But... a month later:

The Queen asked again:

'*Now* who's the happiest one of all? Ha ha!'

'OH, THAT WOULD BE SNOW WHITE STILL. SHE'S MADE FRIENDS WITH THE PRISON GUARDS, TWO MICE AND A COCKROACH. SHE SINGS SONGS, PLAYS THE GUITAR (WHICH HASN'T BEEN INVENTED YET) AND TELLS STORIES TO THE GUARDS, THE MICE AND THE COCKROACH, WHO ALL APPLAUD.'

'Then I'll take her *out* of prison... Let's see... I'll make her *poor* instead! She'll have to live in an old shack with almost no food, and won't be allowed to go to school. She won't be able to take baths, so she'll *stink*! And then she won't have any friends! Ha Ha! Hee Hee! Ho Ho!'

'*THAT* WOULD TEACH HER A LESSON... IF LESSONS HAD BEEN IN-VENTED YET.'

And a *further* month later:

The Queen stood in front of the mirror again:

'Mirror, mirror on the wall, who's the ...'

'SNOW WHITE.'

'You don't know what I was going to ask!'

'I'M A *MAGIC* MIRROR, REMEMBER? SNOW WHITE IS STILL THE HAPPIEST OF ALL. SHE SINGS ALL DAY LONG, AND EVEN THOUGH SHE'S POOR, SHE SHARES HER FOOD WITH AN OLD MAN AND A STRAY KITTEN.'

'Right! I'll have the old man killed. And *you*, Magic Mirror, will use your magic to turn the kitten into an old rat! Ha Ha! Hee Hee! Ho Ho!'

'*THAT* SHOULD TEACH THEM *ALL* A LESSON...'

But next month, the mirror reported that Snow White was still very happy.

'What about the old man?' asked the Queen.

'DEAD, BUT REPLACED BY TWO ORPHANS CALLED HANSEL AND GRETEL. THEY WERE LOOKING FOR A GINGERBREAD HOUSE BUT HAD TO MOVE IN WITH SNOW WHITE INSTEAD.'

'Why?'

'BECAUSE THAT FAIRY TALE HASN'T BEEN INVENTED YET.'

'And the kitten? Did you turn him into a rat?'

'BEFORE I COULD DO THAT, HE TURNED INTO A WHITE RABBIT WEARING A WAISTCOAT AND A POCKET WATCH ON A GOLD CHAIN. HE DISAPPEARED DOWN A RABBIT HOLE PURSUED BY A GIRL CALLED ALICE, WHICH IS VERY ODD INDEED, BECAUSE THAT STORY HASN'T BEEN –'

'Enough of that! What next?'

'I FOUND A RAT TO REPLACE HIM, BUT SNOW WHITE WAS SO KIND TO THE RAT THAT HE'S TAKEN TO CLEAN LIVING. HE SPENDS A LOT OF TIME ON A LITTLE BOAT ON THE RIVER, OR HAVING PICNICS IN THE WOODS WITH HIS FRIENDS BADGER AND MOLE. IT'S MOST STRANGE... '

'Because that story hasn't been invented yet?'

'NO, BECAUSE RATS, BADGERS AND MOLES DON'T USUALLY OWN BOATS.'

The Queen said, 'I've had enough of being kind and good to that girl! There's only one way to deal with Snow White. ... I'll simply have to *kill* her....'

'AH, YES... THAT WILL **DEFINITELY** TEACH HER A LESSON SHE WON'T FORGET...'

Scene 4 In the woods

Three soldiers led Snow White out into the deep, deep woods, arguing about who was to kill her.

'I killed the last one,' the first said.

'But that was a wolf,' said the second.

'*And* we were doing it to save the Three Little Pigs,' said the third.

The first said, 'And it was a good thing we saved them, because they made *lovely* bacon.'

'I can't kill a girl,' said the second soldier. 'Even one that looks like the back end of something that hasn't been invented yet.'

'But if we *don't* kill her,' said the third, 'the Queen might find out and cut our pay, which would *not* be nice. It's either us or the girl, know what I mean?'

The other two soldiers nodded wisely. 'Yeah, we've gotta look after ourselves, right?' they agreed. 'We can't have our pay cut!'

Just then they came to a little clearing in the woods, and they stopped. They tied Snow White to a tree, told her they were sorry, but they would have to kill her. It was just their job, you know.

And Snow White said that was okay, she understood and wouldn't be angry, at least not much. And not for very long.

But just then....

Out from the woods marched seven tough-looking bunnies wearing military camouflage uniforms and carrying machine guns. They pointed their guns at the guards and ordered:

'Untie her!'

The guards stared at the guns and said:

'What are *those*?'

'These are machine guns.'

'But guns haven't been invented yet!'

'So?'

'So… you won't have any bullets to put in them, will you?'

'That's right,' said the toughest of the tough bunnies. 'But we've loaded them with Easter eggs instead. Just think what a hundred Easter eggs at close range will do to your pretty faces!'

'Easter eggs haven't been invented, either!'

'That's what you think, punk.' The Bunny pointed his gun. 'Maybe I invented them last week. You wanna find out? Yeah? Well, what you've gotta ask yourself is this: "*Do I feel lucky?*" Well, do you, punk? Do you feel *lucky*?'

'No.'

'Then untie Snow White and back away reaaaal slow.'

Scene 5 Mirror, mirror…

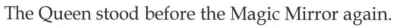

The Queen stood before the Magic Mirror again.

'… who's the fairest of them all?' she asked

'YOU, OF COURSE. BUT ONLY JUST…

    A DARLING GIRL CALLED AMBER ROSE

    WAS GIVEN A MOLE UPON HER NOSE

    BUT THIS SNOZZLE INVENTION

    GETS LOTS OF ATTENTION

    AND EVERYONE LOVES HOW IT GLOWS.'

'Oh, yes? Then I'll turn *her* into a… duck.'

'*THAT* SHOULD DAMPEN HER PROSPECTS…'

'Who's the richest?'

'YOU, QUEENIE BABES!'

'Most famous and glamorous?'

'YOU!'

'Happiest?'

'SNOW WHITE IS STILL THE HAPPIEST OF THEM ALL. SHE LIVES IN A CHARMING TWO-STOREY COTTAGE IN THE NICER END OF THE WOODS, WITH GORGEOUS VIEWS OVER UNSPOILT WOODLANDS. SHE LIVES WITH THE 7 EASTER BUNNIES, HAS HER OWN ROOM ON THE GROUND FLOOR, LOOKS AFTER THEIR CUTE LITTLE GARDEN FULL OF CARROTS AND LETTUCES, AND DOES THEIR CLEANING, COOKING AND WASHING. SHE EVEN HAS A VACUUM CLEANER AND WASHING MACHINE.'

'But those haven't been invented yet!'

'YES, BUT SHE DOESN'T KNOW THAT, SO SHE USES THEM ANYWAY.'

'Then I'll have to take care of her *myself*, won't I?'

'THAT WOULD BE COOL.'

'Being cool hasn't been invented yet. Ha!'

Scene 6 The poisonous apple

The wicked Queen made a poisonous apple. Well, lots of them actually, all piled into a little basket, all beautifully polished, and all looking sweet and scrumptious.

She disguised herself as a nice old lady, which was very, very difficult because she hated old ladies, and she hated NICE old ladies more than almost everything in the world – everything that is, except for Snow White.

Why did the Queen make poisonous apples? Why not kill Snow White with magic, or send lots of soldiers? Because that would be too easy. *And* it would make a very short story.

She turned up one Thursday morning while the 7 Easter Bunnies were out in the mines with their picks and shovels, digging up chocolate to make Easter eggs with.

Snow White was washing their little bunny outfits when a sweet old lady wearing a red hat knocked on the door, then (when there was no answer) banged on the door with an apple (oooh squishy) and then (when there was still no answer) kicked the door with her sweet old lady hobnailed boots.

Snow White opened the door.

'Hello, sweet old lady,' she said. 'I hope our hard door didn't hurt your sweet old toes.'

'That's all right,' said the Wicked Queen. 'Would you like a lovely sweet apple?'

'Apples are gross,' said Snow White. 'Would you like to try one of our special surprise Easter eggs?'

'Yes,' said the Queen. 'But what's the surprise?'

'I don't know,' said Snow White. 'The Bunnies spend a lot of time making things that haven't been invented yet.'

The Queen almost ate the Easter egg. But she paused with it nearly touching her lips. Then she threw it at a tree. The tree exploded.

'Ah yes,' said Snow White. 'That would be the surprise.'

Scene 7 The pretty flowers

The wicked Queen tried again the next day. She prepared some poisoned flowers, and put so much poison in them that just one sniff would kill Snow White. She disguised herself as a different sweet old lady, and turned up the next morning.

Snow White was cooking carrot cake when a sweet old lady wearing a blue hat banged on the door with her blue knuckle-duster, then (when there was no answer) with the flowers (oooh *very* squishy) and then kicked the door with her sweet old lady blue hobnailed boots.

Snow White opened the door.

'Hello, sweet old lady,' she said. 'I hope our hard door didn't hurt your sweet old toes.'

'Hello, little girl. I'm a different old lady from the one who called yesterday.'

'Yes, you are! You're wearing a *blue* hat!' (Snow White was kind and good and sometimes pretty, but she was never smart).

'That's right,' said the Wicked Queen. 'Would you like some pretty flowers? Here, have a gooooood sniff.'

'No, thank you,' said Snow White. 'Flowers make me sneeze. But would you like to try a slice of carrot cake? It's got real carrots in it.'

The Queen had never had carrot cake before, so she said yes, so long as Snow White had ONE sniff of the flowers.

The Queen was just about to have a bite of the cake, and Snow White was just about to have a sniff of the flowers, when the 7 Easter Bunnies burst in through the door, pointed their machine guns at the Wicked Queen, and commanded:

'Back away from the carrot cake, old lady! That's OUR carrot cake!'

'What are you doing here?' the Queen asked. 'Shouldn't you be down at the chocolate mine?'

'We don't work on Fridays,' said the head rabbit. 'Now back away reaaaal slow. These Easter egg bullets are dangerous. And they'd make a mess of the kitchen, which Snow White has just cleaned...'

The Queen dropped the cake and ran out the door, leaving behind one poisoned flower.

'Flower,' said a rabbit.

'Yes,' said Snow White. 'That's what they use in proper cakes, isn't it?' (Snow White was kind and good and sometimes pretty, but let's face it: she was about as dense as a bowl of cold porridge).

Scene 8 The chocolate dessert

The wicked Queen made a wonderful mushy sweet swirly chocolate dessert called a chocolate mousse, with a cherry on top. She knew that there wasn't a woman in the world who could resist chocolate...

She disguised herself as a different old lady, wearing a purple hat this time. It was Monday, and she

was sure there wouldn't be any bunnies around. She knocked on the door, then she banged on it with the cherry (*extremely* squishy!), then …

… she rang the doorbell. But the doorbell made no noise, so she kicked the door with her sweet old lady purple hobnailed boots.

Snow White came and unlocked the door.

'Hello, sweet old lady,' she said. 'I hope our hard door didn't hurt your sweet old toes.'

'Hello, little girl,' the Queen said. 'I'm a different old lady from the one who called on Friday and the day before that.'

'Yes, you are! You're wearing a *purple* hat!' (Snow White was… yes, you've got it, as dim as a 5 watt light bulb).

The Queen asked, 'What's wrong with your doorbell?'

'Doorbells haven't been invented yet. But the bunnies are working on it.'

'That's all right, then,' said the Wicked Queen. 'Would you like some chocolate dessert?'

'Does it have a cherry on top?'

'It used to have,' said the Queen. 'Here's a lovely silver spoon. Go on, have a taste!'

But just then the 7 Easter Bunnies burst in from the kitchen.

'Move away from that chocolate mousse, old lady!' the head bunny ordered. 'WE make the chocolate around here! And by the way, we don't work on Mondays, either!'

'I'm just a sweet old lady who's trying to make

people happy,' whined the Queen.

The bunnies looked at the bowl of chocolate mousse and their noses twitched.

'Okay,' said the head bunny. 'We'll swap. We eat your chocolate, you eat our cake.'

'And what's in the cake?' asked the wicked Queen suspiciously.

Snow White said, 'Butter and sugar and eggs and Flower.'

'No surprises?'

The head Easter Bunny asked, 'Would we trick you? We're just 7 dumb rabbits with machine guns. We don't do surprises, except on Thursdays.'

'Right,' said the Queen. And she took a big bite of Snow White's cake...

... and died.

And Snow White said, 'Oh dear. What a shame! She seemed such a *nice* old lady!' (Snow White was kind and good and sometimes pretty, but... yeah, thick as a brick).

And Snow White took a tiny nibble of the chocolate mousse...

... and fell asleep.

'Oh dear,' said Easter Bunny 1. 'Now we've got to learn to use the washing machine ourselves.'

'And that weird vacuum thing,' said Bunny 2 nervously.

'We'll have to cook our own carrot cake,' said Easter

Bunny 3.

'Wash the floors,' said Bunny 4.

'Do the dusting!' said Bunny 5.

'Yuk!' all the Bunnies exclaimed. They *hated* dust-ing.

'Yeah,' said Easter Bunny 6, 'And we'll have to wait ages for a handsome prince to come and kiss her.'

They looked at one another unhappily. Then Easter Bunny 7 said, 'Or one of us could kiss her instead. You know, cut out the middle man.'

SO…

The head Easter Bunny kissed Snow White, who woke up and married him… because even though he was a bunny, he was a good kisser.

They lived happily ever after, she as the good and kind but not very clever Queen who sang all day, looked after her people and made them happy; he as the good and kind Easter Bunny who looked after all the children in the kingdom and made them Easter eggs shaped like
    rabbits
       toys

       baby chicks
       and cartoon characters…

… even though they hadn't been invented yet.

The Fairy and the Horse

The voices

Maureen the Irish Fairy has a lovely musical voice. I expect she comes from somewhere near Galway, and therefore she tends to pronounce "th" as if has almost no "h" in it at all. She is always kind and generous herself, and is somewhat puzzled that not everyone is like that. She's a very sensible fairy, but not dull with it: there's always a hint of a laugh in her fine Irish fairy voice.

The **Witch** is a nasty piece of work, and proud of it. She really enjoys being a witch, especially the dressing up. She does have the most beautiful hair you've ever seen, a pretty face, nice body and lovely fingernails; but you shouldn't let things like that fool you. After all, most witches are drop-dead gorgeous. (What? You thought that a woman with magical powers would somehow forget to use her powers to make herself beautiful? It's the *first* thing she would do!). As for her voice, she makes herself sound completely charming when she's tricking the Horse, but for most of this story she gloats and cackles and sneers to her heart's content.

The **Horse** talks with a bit of a whinny and a lot of a lisp (for instance he says "danth" for "dance"). He sounds silly. He *is* silly, in an irrepressibly bouncy sort of way, rather like Tigger from 'Winnie the Pooh'. He really does believe that he's the best dancer in the world, and is waiting excitedly for a phone call inviting him to appear on "Thelebrity Come Dan-thing".

The story

Once upon a time there was an Irish fairy named Maureen. On a fine summer's day she went for a walk in the woods, not knowing that she had wandered into a witch's domain.

She had come to the edge of a grassy clearing and was about to climb the low hill in front of her, when an arm came out from the nettles and grabbed her.

'Ha Ha!' cried the Witch. 'Gotcha!'

The Witch was tall and strong, and had long black hair beneath a high, pointed witch's hat. She had a beautiful face and was dressed in black silk.

'That's a very nice hat you have there,' said Maureen politely. 'And your hair is *lovely*. Which shampoo do you use?'

But all the Witch did was laugh and push the fairy into a big sack, so that she was upside down with her feet sticking out of the top. The Fairy tried to use her wand, but since she was in the Witch's lands, her magic was about as useful as a bald man's hairbrush.

The Witch tied the sack to a tree and poked beetles, earwigs, caterpillars, slugs, snails, ants, scorpions and centipedes into it.

'Please don't do that,' Maureen asked from inside the sack. 'It's rather unkind, you know, especially since I'm upside down. All the little creatures fall to the bottom of the sack and crawl about my head.'

'I'll teach you to trespass in *my* woods!' the Witch shouted. 'How d'you like those slugs, hey?'

'I don't like them at all,' said Maureen. 'They're

making a mess of my hair, and I spent hours styling it this morning.'

'Are you complaining?' screeched the Witch. 'Well, here's what we witches do to fairies who complain – we whack them with our special fairy-whacking brooms!' And with her right hand she began hitting the sack with her thick witch's broom.

'*OW!* I'm *not* complaining,' said the Fairy. 'I was simply answering your question about the slugs!'

'Ha!' cried the Witch. 'You trample all over my woods, and all you can do is moan about the wild-life? Well, here's what we witches do to fairies who moan – we whip them with our wands!'

And with her left hand she began hitting the sack with her witch's wand, which was made from the thorny stem of a rosebush.

'I do – *OW!* – apologise – *YIII!*,' said the Fairy, as the broom whacked her on one side and the wand whipped her on the other. 'I – *yikes!* - didn't know – *OUCH!* – that these were *your* woods. Do you think you could at least – *would you please stop that?* - take the earwigs out? They're rather tickly, don't you know.'

'Take something *out*?' the Witch scoffed. 'For that complaint, I'll put something else *in*! I know - I'll go get some red-hot coals from my fireplace!'

The Greatest Dancer in the World

As the Witch sped away back to her house, Maureen heard an odd sound. It seemed to be a horse, but whereas most horses went *clip*-clop-*clip*-clop, this one was going *clip-clip*-clop-clop-*clip*-clop-clop.

Then it went *clip*-clop-*clip* (pause) clop-*clip*-clop (pause) for a while. And she heard something talking to itself in a very horsey whinny:

'I'm the greatetht danther in the world!'

She peeked through a small hole in the sack and saw a large brown horse skipping sidewards - and rather clumsily - down the little hill above her.

He paused at a low wooden fence and leaned against it, still talking to himself. 'Thlow, thlow, quick quick thlow... or wath it Thlow, quick quick thlow, quick quick? Or –'

But he leaned over a little too much, and the fence broke. He rolled down the hillside all the way to the edge of the woods and ended up quite close to where the Fairy was hanging upside down in the Witch's sack.

'Help!' the Fairy cried. And then, remembering her manners, she introduced herself. 'I'm Maureen the Irish Fairy. Who are you?'

'I'm a horthee!'

'Please help me, Mister Horsey!' the Fairy begged.

'Oh...' The Horse sounded disappointed. 'Don't you want to thee me danth first?'

'I don't think so,' she said.

'I do a fine foxtrot.'

'I'm sure you do, but you see –'

'My tango is motht extraordinary.'

'Yes, but there's not much time for that –'

'I'm the greatetht danther in the whole world!'

'Oh, no you're not! I've *seen* you dance!'

The Horse was most offended. 'Not *properly*,' he said. 'I was jutht fooling about up there. Look, I'll do a little cha-cha-cha for you. Left, right, left-left right, right, left, right-right left... Thee?'

Maureen asked, laughing, 'That was *dancing*, was it? It looked more like a three-legged spider hopping on hot coals!'

'Really? Wath I *that* good? You are thoooo thweet! Wanna thee my Rumba next?'

The Fairy sighed. 'Look, Horsey,' she said, 'if you help me quickly, I'll give you one wish.'

'All right, then. I've alwayth wanted one of them!'

'First you'll have to free me from this sack.'

'No problem, thweetie.' And the Horse bit through the rope that fastened the Witch's sack to the tree. The sack fell to the ground and the Fairy landed on her head.

'OW!' she exclaimed. 'That was my head! *And* my hair! It's all tangled now!'

She wriggled out of the sack and dusted herself down. She pulled a special fairy hairbrush from a pocket and began untangling her hair as she talked.

'Now, Horsey, we must get out of the Witch's lands before she comes back. Then I'll be able to use my magic and give you the one wish I agreed.'

'Don't you want to thee my Thaltha firtht?'

'Your Salsa? No, not if it's anything like your Cha-cha-cha.'

She leapt onto the Horse's back. 'Let's go,' she said.

The Horse asked, 'Do you want me to go *this* way?' (*little waltz*) 'Or *this* way?' (*little skip*) 'Or –'

'Just go *fast*!' (*whack!*)

'Ohhhh… *that'th* not nithe!'

The Horse shot off up the hillside at a fast pace, but as he approached the big ditch which marked the boundary of the Witch's domain, he shouted back over his shoulder, 'Watch thith! I'm going to jump it thidewayth!'

'Why?'

'Because it lookth nither!'

The Horse made it *most* of the way across the ditch, but fell into the deep mud… as did the Fairy.

She landed flat on her back in the ditch. 'You great eejut!' she shouted, pounding the mud with her fists. 'Look at me now! I'm *covered* in mud! And what about my lovely Irish fairy curls? They're *ruined*!'

They crawled out of the ditch and sat at the top, not knowing that the Witch had come back and was listening to them from behind a hedge.

The Fairy said, 'At least we're out of the Witch's woods now, and I can do magic again. You've coated me in mud quite un- necessarily, but I did promise you a wish… so what do you want, Horsey?'

The Horse gave an excited whinny. 'Well, I *had* thought I wanted to eat the betht grath in the whole wide world, but I *altho* want to be able to fly. And I think that if I can fly, I will go and find the betht grath anyway!'

Behind the hedge, the Witch rubbed her hands with evil glee. She watched as the Fairy pulled out her wand (which was made from a delicate bluebell) and then - *ping coppowwee!* – two wings sprouted from the Horse's shoulders.

'Yippee!' The Horse began leaping about, flapping its wings and spinning in the air. 'I can fly! I can fly!'

The Fairy watched him cavorting in the air above.

He dropped to the ground and offered, 'I know! I can give you a ride home!'

The Fairy said firmly, 'No, you won't. If you fly the way you dance, I'll be *much* safer on the ground.'

'But I'm the betht danther in the world!

'Oh, no you're not.'

'Oh yeth I *am*! I jutht need practith! But the lady hortheth won't danth with me...'

'You're probably not asking them nicely.'

'I thay *very* nithe thingth to them.'

'Such as?'

'*You got a lovely pair of hooveth.* And then I thay, *For a big girl, you don't thweat much!*'

'And they don't like that?' the Fairy laughed.

'And then I thay, *Nithe tail you got there!*'

'I suppose it might work with a horse. But it certainly wouldn't work with a fairy.'

'Oh, come on! Fly with me!'

'I think you ought to go look for your grass,' the

Fairy suggested. 'And *I* will go home and wash my hair. Once you've found your grass, come to my fairy hideout and I'll have one ride. Only one, mind you – and NO dancing!'

The Fairy whispered in the Horse's ear how to find her fairy house, then waved her bluebell wand again, and disappeared.

The Witch laughed to herself and crept away quietly. She went home and turned her broom into…

… a lawnmower!

The Witch's Trick

The Horse flew away and spent a happy hour circling about looking for good grass. Then he noticed in the middle of woods a dear little house with a big grassy green lawn in front, into which was cut the message:

𝕿𝖍𝖊 𝖇𝖊𝖘𝖙 𝖌𝖗𝖆𝖘𝖘 𝖎𝖓 𝖙𝖍𝖊 𝖜𝖍𝖔𝖑𝖊 𝖜𝖎𝖉𝖊 𝖜𝖔𝖗𝖑𝖉

He was ecstatic! He landed in the middle of this beautiful field of lush grass and was about to start eating when he saw a sign:

> Please knock on door before eating grass.

The door was opened by a tall lady with beautiful black hair and a pointed hat.

'Yes?' the Witch asked. 'Who are you?'

The Horse neighed. 'It ith I, the greatetht danther in

the world! And now I'm altho the greatetht flier!'

'I see,' said the Witch with a wicked smile. 'You're a *horse* – and you *fly* – so *now* you're a… *horsefly*!'

She waved her thorny wand and - *ping coppowwee!* - the Horse shrank to the size of a common horsefly. She caught him in a glass jar and took him into her house.

'Now, little horsefly, what shall I do with you?' the Witch asked cruelly. 'Should I let my pet froggy play with you?'

She carried the jar to a patch of slime in a corner of the room and showed it to the large, ugly frog squatting there. The frog hopped close and began licking the outside of the jar hungrily with its long, sticky tongue.

'Oh, pleath no!' pleaded the Horse in its tiny, buzzy horsefly voice. 'Don't feed me to the frog!'

'Or should I give you to my pet spider?' the Witch wondered.

She stood on a chair and held the jar next to a web hanging from the ceiling above the frog. A big, hairy spider leapt upon the jar and tried to unscrew the lid with its strong legs.

'Not the thpider! Pleath not the thpider!' the Horse cried out.

'Or what about a swim with my little fishes, mister horsefly?'

The Witch dropped the jar into the water of the fish tank, where it bobbed to and fro as several fish with big teeth and nasty looks in their fishy eyes headbutted the glass jar, trying to break it.

'I can't thwim! 'Help! Pleath don't let the fish get me!'

The Witch smiled wickedly to herself. But then she put on a sad face and said in an unhappy voice, 'It's so hard being a witch. We don't have any friends, you know. And *nobody* trusts us.'

The horsefly gave a hopeful buzz and said, 'That'th very thad… Um… *I'll* be your friend, if you like!'

'Really? You know, I'm getting tired of being nasty all the time. Maybe I should try to change…'

'Oh, you should! You should!'

'Ohhhhh… all right, then. But if I turn you back into a horse, you must promise never to let that Fairy know I've done so.'

'I promith!'

'You see, if you tell the Fairy I caught you and then let you go, she'll think I've gone soft and won't respect me any longer. And I couldn't take that. I would turn nasty again, and I would have to come find you. And then my little froggy and spider and fishes would have a lovely meal. I'd probably give them a bite each.'

'I won't tell, really I won't!'

'Good! So, not one word to her about any of this!'

The Witch took the horsefly outside, waved her thorny wand, and - *coppowee!* - he was a horse again.

He exclaimed, 'Oh, thank you!' He was so pleased to be a horse again that he did a little dance.

'Wait a minute!' said the Witch. 'You seem to have something wrong with your left hind hoof.'

'Have I?'

The Witch lifted his hoof and pretended to poke at it with her wand. But she was really tying a strand of her hair to it.

It was the most wonderful hair - long, silky and black; and it was so fine that if you held an individual strand of it before your eyes, you couldn't see it.

'There!' the witch said. 'All fixed now!'

She gave the horse a pat on the top of his back next, as if being friendly... but she was really putting something very sticky up there... the sort of very strong stickiness you might find on a spider's web.

'Off you go, then!' she cried. 'And remember – not a word to the Fairy!'

Taken for a Ride...

The Horse flew to the secret hideaway of the Fairy, not noticing the strand of hair attached to his hoof. The Witch stood in the doorway of her house, laughing, as her hair unravelled until she was left almost bald.

The Horse landed at the Fairy's house and pawed at the door with a front hoof.

'I'm here!' he shouted.

The Fairy opened the door. 'There's no need to kick the door in,' she said.

'Thorry about that. But it'th time for our little flight! Aren't you exthited?'

'No,' said the Fairy, 'but I *am* worried.'

'Oh. You think you'll fall off?'

'It's not that. I'm worried about my hair getting tangled in the wind.' She tied a scarf over her head and climbed onto the Horse's back.

'Come on, then,' she said. 'But don't go into any clouds. I don't like getting my hair wet.'

The Horse flew up and away… and then sidewards and away… and then backwards…

'That's really rather clever,' said Maureen the Fairy. 'Even *I* can't fly backwards this quickly!'

'Am I going backwardth?' asked the Horse in a puzzled way. 'I wath *trying* to go forwardth!'

Of course, what was happening was that the Witch was reeling in the Horse. And as she pulled the hair into her house she was turning it into a very large…

… spider's web!

The web soon covered the ceiling of the Witch's front room, and the Witch hummed to herself as she pulled in the rest of the hair and stuck it back onto her head.

Meanwhile, up in the sky, the Fairy was saying:

'I think I'll get off now. Please go down to the ground.'

'I can't!' exclaimed the Horse. 'Thomething'th got me!'

'Then I'll *jump* off and fly back.' The Fairy tried to stand up on the Horse's back. But she was stuck fast by the glue the Witch had patted there.

'All right,' she said. 'I *won't* jump off. I'll simply magic us back to my house.' But as soon as she raised her bluebell wand and saw that it had turned into a *purplebell* wand instead, she knew it wasn't going to work.

'Oh no!' she exclaimed. 'We must be over the

Witch's lands!'

'Oh well,' said the Horse. 'At leatht there'll be thome good grath to eat here...'

'What?' cried the Fairy. 'How do you know that? Have you been here already?'

'Oh,' said the Horse sheepishly (which by the way is very difficult for a horse to do), 'I wathn't thup-pothed to mention that...'

Just then they were dragged down to the Witch's house, and pulled right through the open front door and into the middle of the front room.

And in the web above, waiting for them, was the Witch, looking very like a big spider with lovely long black hair.

'Ha ha!' she cried. 'Gotcha again!'

She snatched the Fairy off the Horse's back and pulled her up onto the web.

'And look, dearie!' she exclaimed. 'I've got a big fire going, so there's plenty of red hot coals for you this time!'

'You're a very, *very* horrid person,' said Maureen the Fairy, 'even though you have such nice hair.'

The Witch paused from tying the Fairy to the web. 'You think *this* is horrid?' she asked. 'Just you wait! I've some even nastier surprises planned for *you*!'

She looked down from the web at the Horse and said, 'You can go, you stupid animal. It was a pleas-ure tricking you.'

'No!' shouted the Horse. 'Let the fairy go! Have *me* inthtead!'

'Nah. I don't fancy horse blood when there's sweet fairy blood to suck.'

Tarantella
...which you may know is a dance connected with the tarantula

The Horse began doing an angry dance. He managed to look annoyed and silly at the same time, jumping about, kicking up his heels, and neighing loudly.

The Witch was furious. 'Stop that!' she shouted. 'How can I concentrate on my evil spells if you're prancing about? And look – you're making holes in my lovely new carpet!'

'I *won't* thtop!' insisted the Horse. 'Not until you let the Fairy go!'

'I've changed my mind,' said the Witch, scuttling upside down along her web towards the Horse. There was an evil look on her face. 'I think I *will* have a little horse blood as an appetiser. Ha ha!'

She let herself down from the web on a strand of web hair.

'Stupid horse!' she hissed. 'If you'd flown off, you'd be safe. But *now* you're going to be a tasty little snack!'

'Thtupid?' asked the Horse. '*Me* thtupid? No, it'th *YOU!*'

And he whirled about so that he had his rear towards the Witch, and then he gave her an enormous kick.

'OWWWW!'

The Witch-spider swung on her strand of hair up to the ceiling, where she smacked up against a hard wooden beam.

'OUCH!'

She swung down again. The Horse was waiting for her.

KICK

   'OWWWWWWWW!'

      SWING

         'OUUUUUCH!

      SWING

KICK

   'OWWWWWWWW!'

      SWING

         'OUUUUUCH!

      SWING

KICK

… And so on, until the strand of hair broke with all the kicking and swinging, and the Witch plopped onto the floor.

KICK!

   'YIIIIIII!'

The Witch sailed through the air and landed in the fire – that lovely hot fire she had built especially high so there would be plenty of red hot coals to bother the Fairy with.

   'OwOwOwOwOwwwwwwwww!'

'Quick!' shouted the Fairy down to the Horse. 'Bite through the web and set me free. But not –

   - *Ouch!*'

The Fairy landed on her head. 'But *not* so that I fall on my head,' she finished. 'You've ruined my lovely Irish fairy curls *again!*'

She leapt up and grabbed the Witch's broom, which had given up being a lawnmower and was creeping out of the door all by itself. She threw it into the fire, followed by the Witch's thorny wand.

'Let's go!' she shouted as flames began spouting from the fireplace. She leapt onto the Horse's back.

The Horse asked, 'Do you want me to go *this* way?' *(little tango)* 'Or *this* way?' *(little foxtrot)* 'Or –'

'Just go *fast*!' *(whack!)*

'Ohhhh… *that'th* not nithe!'

They flew out of the door and sped away from the burning house. The Horse flew the Fairy back to her own home.

'Thank you, Horsey!' said the Fairy as she climbed off. She gave him a little kiss on the nose.

'Ohhhh - that'th *nithe*! Can I marry you?'

'I can't marry a horse!'

'Can't you turn me into handthome prince and *then* marry me?'

'No,' said Maureen the Irish Fairy. 'If I married you, I would have to dance with you at the wedding party, and I'll *never* do that – I've *seen* you dance.'

'But I'm the greatetht danther in the world!'

'Oh, no you're not!'

Mouldysocks
and the Three Humans

The voices

The best way to read this story is in a gruff bear voice. Sorry, I mean *Duh best wayta read dis story is inna gruff bear voice.* If you want to know how bears speak, you could try reading a book of mine called "Bullies", where this little tale is told throughout in *Bear Talk.*

Daddy Human sounds very much like a well-to-do father from some leafy village. He probably works "in the City", reads the Financial Times on the train there, and carries a neatly-rolled dark umbrella which matches his dark grey suit. He is rather clever at work, and rather stupid at anything practical such as tying his shoes.

Mummy Human is one of those very proper, well-spoken ladies who like things to be neat and tidy. She's not particularly bright. Her cooking is terrible, but that's okay because the family usually eat at restaurants anyway. All she has to do is make breakfast. Porridge. Again.

For some reason, once **Baby Human** starts talking properly, he speaks with a cockney accent, no doubt to the great surprise of his parents. He probably got this from watching East Enders on television. Until he starts talking, he gabbles nonsense words in a most amusing little voice. If you've ever heard the Goon Show, his voice is somewhere between *Bluebottle* and *Little Jim*. His "pretend words" are quite musical and usually go up on the last syllable, such as the first thing he says: "Eh-*deh*, eh-bud*duh*a*duh*".

Mouldysocks lets his actions speak for themselves. He's determined to find simple and clever solutions to life's problems, and to bring kindness and justice to tricky situations. When he does so, he's quite likely to acknowledge the audience's storming applause by saying quietly and humbly, 'I'm just that kind of bear, you know?'

Note: Bears are of course quite biased against Humans and regard them all as "stoopid", even when they aren't. But you can't really blame the bears for that. After all, bears haven't filled the world with rubbish, pollution, poverty, global warming and terrible wars – the "Hoomuns" did that.

The story

Wuns upon a time, dere wuz free Hoomuns:
  Daddy Hoomun
  Mummy Hoomun
  And stoopid liddle Baby Hoomun!

… I'd better start again.

You may know the story of Goldilocks and the Three Bears. *The bears don't like that story*!
They have their own version, which in Bear Talk is pronounced "Mouldysocks an duh Free Hoomuns". Here it is, in what the bears would call *Hoomun Tawk*.

Once upon a time there were Three Humans –
Mummy Human
Daddy Human
and stupid little Baby Human.
Now, Baby Human wasn't stupid for a human. But he was *very* stupid for a bear. He was so stupid that, even though he was two years old, he couldn't climb a tree to find honey! Even the smallest bear could do that! It just goes to show how stupid humans are...
One day, the Three Humans woke up and came downstairs for breakfast.
Porridge *again*.
They always had porridge. It was the only thing Mummy Human knew how to make!

So they sat down at the table, and Daddy Human picked up his...
... fork! Yes, he was *that* stupid!
Mummy Human picked up her spoon and Baby Human picked up *his* spoon, and then - you won't believe this bit, I know – then, just as they were about to eat their porridge, Daddy Human said:
'Let's go for a walk, shall we?'
Now, if Mummy Human was a bear, she would have stuck the porridge pan upside down on his big, stupid head. But being a Human, she just said, 'Oh, what a *lovely* idea!'
And Baby Human looked sadly at his porridge and said in his little voice, 'Eh-deh, eh-buddubaduh!' ...

... because that's about all he ever said.

The Walk

So off they went. But as soon as they got to the garden gate, Baby Human looked down and said:

'Ehhhh... Dudda pittah pudeepa dabudda!' - which
means, *'We forgot to put our boots on!'*

And Daddy Human looked down and said
thoughtfully, 'Oh, yes...'

And Mummy Human looked down and said
firmly, 'Oh, no!'

And so they went back to the house, put their boots
on, and THEN they went for a walk!

This time they got halfway to the village before
Baby Human looked down again and said:

'Ehhhhh! Debudupah debah deboo eepududda
dabba supaduba bootabah!' - which means, *'We put
our boots on, but we forgot to put our socks on!'*

And Daddy Human looked down and said, 'Oh,
yes...'

And Mummy Human looked down and said, 'Oh,
no!'

And so they went back home, took their boots off,
put their socks on, put their boots on, and THEN
they went for a walk!

Now, it was Sunday. This time they got all the way
to the village church, just as people were coming
out. And Baby Human looked down again and said
with a little scream:

'Agh! Dah puttabar bahdeebuhdee sibodabah
diboodie pittabapuddee suppabadeeta!' - which

means, *'We put our boots on…*

… and we put our socks on…

*… but we forgot to put our **clothes** on!'*

And Daddy Human looked down and said slowly, 'Oh… yes…'

And Mummy Human looked down and screamed, 'OH, NO!!'

And they RAN back home, took their boots off, put their clothes on, and FINALLY they went for a walk!

This time they decided not to go past the church again, and went into the forest instead. And after a while, Baby Human looked down and said sadly,

'Ah! Mahtah dittah, bootah dabba!' - which means, *'We forgot to put our boots on again!'*

And Daddy Human and Mummy Human both said, 'Tough!'

Back at the Cottage…

While the humans were away, a good, upright, intelligent bear named Mouldysocks came to their house.

He knocked on the door, but there was no reply. And Mouldysocks knew that if you knock on someone's door, and there's no answer, you *don't* just open the door and go in, do you?

Of course not!

That's the sort of thing a Human like Goldilocks would do, right?

Mouldysocks didn't try to open the door. *He* went in by the window instead!

And there on the table were three bowls of porridge. First, he tried Daddy Human's porridge.

Too hot!

Pwwwt! He had to spit it out!

Then he tried Mummy Human's porridge.

Too cold!

Pwwwt! He had to spit that out, too!

Lastly, he tried Baby Human's porridge. And Baby Human's porridge was just right, so he ate it all up. With a whole jar of honey on top of it. Of course.

Then, being a clever bear, he took Daddy Human's porridge (which was too hot) and Mummy Human's porridge (which was too cold) and mixed them together...

... and then *they* were both just right too, so he ate *them* as well. With all the sugar from the sugar bowl. Of course!

Then, because he liked Baby Human's spoon and bowl (they had pictures of bears on them), he washed them up and put them away.

'I'm just that kind of bear,' he said.

Next he went into the next room, where there were three chairs.

First he sat on Daddy Human's chair, but it was too hard. So he fetched the pan of porridge from the kitchen and spread some porridge on Daddy Human's chair.

'That'll make it softer!' he said.

Then he sat on Mummy Human's chair, but it was too soft. So he found her pincushion and pushed all her pins and needles into the chair seat.

'That'll make it harder!' he said.

Lastly, he looked at Baby Human's chair. Now, you need to know something about this chair. Every night of every week for the last month, Mummy Human had said to Daddy Human:

'Daddy! You need to do something about Baby's chair. It's falling to pieces, and Baby can't sit in it!'

And every night of every week, Daddy Human said, 'Oh, yes... I'll do something about it at the weekend.'

But he never did. Daddy Humans are like that.

Now, Mouldysocks didn't know this, so he sat in Baby Human's chair - and it broke into little pieces! So he put them on the fire...

But he felt sorry for Baby Human, so he went and found Daddy Humans' credit card...

... and phoned a chair shop...

... and ordered *two* big leather chairs for Baby Human, the kind that recline and have little refrigerators built into the arms.

'I'm just that kind of bear,' he said.

Then he went upstairs, and there were three beds. Daddy Human's bed was too hard: so he bounced on it for a long time.

'That'll make it softer!' he said.

Mummy Human's bed was too soft, and Baby Human's bed wasn't right, either: so he picked up Baby Human's bed and put it on top of Mummy Human's bed, and then it was just right.

So he climbed in and went to sleep.

Return of the Humans

The Three Humans came back up the path, and Daddy Human knocked on the door. There was no answer.

'Oh dear...' he said. 'It appears that no one is at home.'

Mummy Human knocked on the door, but there was still no answer. And *she* said, 'We'll have to come back later.'

And off they went down the path again, leaving Baby Human (who wasn't as stupid as he looked) standing alone by the front door. And Baby Human whistled to Mummy Human and Daddy Human and pointed at the door and shouted,

'Ay! E-yah! Oi! Oi!!' – which means, *'It's our house, innit?'*

So the Three Humans went inside and sat at the breakfast table.

Daddy Human picked up his… fork… and said, 'Someone's been licking my fork!'

And Mummy Human picked up her spoon and said, 'Someone's been licking my spoon!'

And Baby Human stared at the table and said, 'Hey! Where's me spoon gone?'

And those were the first proper words he'd ever spoken.

Then Daddy Human looked at his bowl and said, 'Someone's been eating my porridge!'

And Mummy Human looked at *her* bowl and said, 'Someone's been eating *my* porridge!'

And Baby Human looked at…

    … the table…

        … and under the table…

            … and said, 'Where's me *bowl* gone?'

And Daddy Human said, 'I know! We must have eaten our porridge before we went for our walk…'

And Mummy Human said, '*And* we must have spat a lot of it out onto the table, too!'

So they got up and went into the next room, and Daddy Human sat down on his chair. It went *Phlutt-pwwwwt-sqshhh!* and he leapt up and said slowly, 'Someone's done something to my chair!'

And Mummy Human sat down on *her* chair and then leapt up again and said, '*Ooh!* Someone's done something to *my* chair!'

And Baby Human looked all around the room warily and said, 'Where's me *CHAIR* gone?'

Then they went upstairs to the bedroom. Daddy Human looked at his bed and said, 'Someone's done something to my bed!'
And Mummy Human said, 'Someone's done something to MY bed!'
And Baby Human looked around in desperation and moaned, 'Where's me *BED* gone?!!'

Just then they saw Mouldysocks. And Daddy Human said, 'It's Mouldysocks!'
And Mummy Human said, 'It's Mouldysocks!'
And Baby Human said, '*Where's* me bed gone???'

Then Daddy Human ran downstairs and got a big gun!
And Mummy Human ran downstairs and got a big knife!
And Baby Human ran downstairs and got...
... a big packet of cookies!
'You *stupid* baby!' shouted Daddy Human. 'Go get something FRIGHTENING!'
And Baby Human ran downstairs and got...
... a photograph of Mummy...
... wearing a swimsuit!
And Daddy Human shouted, 'No! Not *THAT* frightening!'

Just then Mouldysocks woke up.
Daddy Human pointed the gun and said, 'Say your

prayers, Mouldysocks!'

And Mummy Human pointed the knife and said, 'Say your prayers, Mouldysocks!'

And Baby Human pointed the… photograph of Mummy… and said, 'Ah... errhum... want a cookie, Mouldysocks?'

And Mouldysocks knew he was cornered. But, being a clever, resourceful and good little bear who always said his prayers, he simply lay back in bed…

… pulled up the covers …

… and showed them his mouldy socks.

And Daddy Human said 'Phew!' and fainted.
And Mummy Human said 'Poohee!' and fainted.
And Baby Human said, 'Where's… me…. bed… gone?' and fainted.

And Mouldysocks said to himself as he walked away into the forest, 'Well, they don't call me Mouldysocks for nothing!'

An dat's duh end uv duh story.

The Boy and the Trolls

The voices

The **Father and Mother** talk just like your own parents did when you were little. They sound a little tired just now, because the boy's baby sister keeps them up at night. That might explain why they don't listen to the boy as carefully as they should.

The **Boy** is a determined little fellow who talks to himself a lot because no one listens to him at home. He has a pleasant little voice, and even when he's complaining about his sister getting all the attention, he doesn't whine. He does sound quite annoyed and puzzled by life, which is understandable.

The **Worm** has a thin, sibilant voice like that of a small and friendly snake.

The **Beetle** sounds most discontented, probably because of the unexpected fall in leg count.

The **Slug** just sounds relieved, in a slow, slippery way.

The **Baby Birds** are greedy and shrill. They have long necks, big eyes and razor sharp beaks. They are forever quarrelling with one another and only ever say nice things when they think they might get some food as a result.

The **Trolls** are the stupidest creatures imaginable, and talk like it. They spend all day watching TV, and only see one channel because they don't know how to change it. They also have quite a nasty streak. Imagine any brainless thug from the movies; that's what they sound like. The **Baby Troll** is slightly brighter than the others, and is content with the one thing he understands: biting.

The story

Once upon a time there was a boy who had a very annoying baby sister. His mother and father thought she was *wonderful*. But they were wrong! She was a real pain! But what really upset him was that *she* got all the attention…

One morning at breakfast, his father was reading the newspaper and his mother was playing with his little sister, who was sitting in her high chair.

The boy said, 'Nobody loves me! Nobody cares!'

His father was busy reading and didn't really hear him. He just said, 'Mmmm. Yes… Mmmm.'

His mother was too busy feeding the baby sister

and playing with her. She just said, 'Really? That's nice, dear...'

So the boy jumped up from the table and shouted, I'm running away! Don't try to stop me!'

And his father turned to the next page in his newspaper and said, 'That's interesting... Mmmm.'

His mother said, 'Really? That's nice, dear...'

So the boy ran out of the door and through the gate and down the road as fast as he could go. And all he took with him was:

    ≋ a book he couldn't read, and

    ☠ a sausage that wasn't cooked.

He ran and ran and ran, until his legs were tired and the sun was high in the sky. And he said as he ran, 'They don't love me! They don't even *listen* to me! All they care about is HER! So I'm running away!'

After a while, he felt so tired he simply *had* to walk. And he said to himself, 'Well, okay, *sometimes* they listen to me...

    ... but I'm STILL running away!'

Finally he began to get hungry. So he took out the sausage and... and it was all raw and slimy, so he threw it away and walked on.

And he said to himself, 'Well, *sometimes* the food at home is better than raw sausages...

    ... but I'm STILL running away!'

An hour later, he was so hungry that he wished he had the sausage back. Then he came to a stream and had a drink of water. He dug into the soft sand at the side of the stream and found a very slippery, very loooooonnngggg earthworm. He held it up and asked, 'I wonder if earthworms are good to eat?'

He puzzled over the two ends and said, 'But which end is the right one to start on? I know, I'll just have a little suck of this end…

… OH YUKKKK! WRONG END!'

He turned the worm around and tried the other end instead.

'OH YUKKKK! IT'S GOT *TWO* WRONG ENDS!'

So he put it down, saying, 'That was *disgusting*!'

And the worm said as it wriggled away, 'It was pretty disgusting for *me*, too!'

… An hour later, he was so hungry that he wished he had the worm back. So he turned over some logs and found an enormous black beetle. He held it up and asked, 'I wonder if beetles are good to eat?'

He said, 'I'll just have a nibble of one leg…

… OH YUKKKK! ARGHHHH! UGH!!!'

And he put it down, saying, 'That was *horrible*!'

And the beetle said as it limped away on five legs, 'It was pretty horrible for *me*, too!'

… An hour later, he was so hungry that he wished he had the beetle back. He started turning over some rocks and found a huge, grey, slimy slug. He held it up and asked, 'I wonder if slugs are good to eat?'

And he looked at the slug, and the slug looked at him. And the boy put it down, saying, 'I think that would be *revolting*!'

And the slug said as it slimed away back under a

rock, 'It would have been pretty revolting for *me* as well!'

And the boy said to himself, 'Well, actually, home was usually better than this. I had real food to eat, and real people to talk to instead of slugs and beetles and worms...

... but I'm STILL running away!'

So he started running again, as the sun climbed down from the top of the sky back to the edge of the wild world. And as darkness fell, the boy looked around and realised that he was...

... LOST.

And then it started to rain. Soon it was so dark that he had to walk with his hands stretched out in front of him, stumbling onwards through the cold, cold rain, his teeth chattering and his hair dripping.

And he said as he walked, 'Home was never *this* bad. It was always dry and warm there. You know, if I could find my way home again, I'd be much nicer to everyone... I might even kiss my little sister!'

As he walked on, he came to a little hill covered with a feathery grass. He crawled in amongst the grass, and found it kept the rain off him. He crawled to the top of the hill, curled up and fell asleep....

BAD mistake!

When he woke the next morning, he heard an un-

usual noise. He lay there with his eyes closed, feeling the sunshine and the breeze, and listening to this odd, odd sound, repeated without pause:
WWWUMF! WWWUMF! WWWUMF!

He opened one eye. He was looking up into the clouds, which seemed *very* close. He opened the other eye. Some of the clouds floated past him. He stood up…

And the wind knocked him over!

What was going on? He stood up again, more carefully this time. He looked down at the feathery grass about his feet.

It was feathery, but it wasn't grass. It was *feathers*. He was standing on the back of an enormous bird!

It was a bird the size of a small house. Behind him was a feathery tail; to the left and right, two great wings were pumping up and down:
WWWUMF! WWWUMF! WWWUMF!

And in front of him was a head shaped like that of a great, hungry hawk. In its curved beak it carried what he first thought were long, wiggling worms. But that must be wrong… No! They were enormous serpents, each of them several metres long.

'I must get off!' the boy said, and he stepped carefully towards the back of the bird. But when he looked over the edge, he saw how far the ground was below him. He could imagine himself stepping off the bird and falling, falling, falling, falling, falling…..

'No, I won't!' he said, and quickly sat down again.

The Birds

The bird was flying towards some high mountains.

'I know those mountains!' the boy exclaimed. 'Those are the mountains I can see from our house! And look – there *is* my house, down there! Hi, Mum! … Oh... Bye, Mum…'

And the boy said, 'It's quite a nice house, really. Even my baby sister is okay *sometimes*. If I ever get home again, I'll definitely give everyone a big hug and never run away again. And I might even give my little sister a kiss.'

The bird flew on, over the boy's house and around the side of the mountains. Higher and higher it flew, and colder and colder the wind became. Then the bird flew straight towards the side of a very high cliff. There was a big hole in the cliff, and the bird flew into it.

The bird landed inside the cave and the boy looked around. There was a little ledge just above him and he pulled himself onto it. He hid behind some rocks and watched.

There was a big nest just inside the cave, and in the nest were three very ugly, very large baby birds, all screeching and fighting for the scraps of serpent that the mother bird threw them.

'That's *my* breakfast!' hissed the biggest one, snatching some snake from the middle one.

'And that's *my* breakfast!' screeched the middle one, snatching snake from the littlest.

'I got *no* breakfast at all!' the littlest complained in a sad little voice. But it was lying, because the mother had thrown it the nicest bits, which it was hiding underneath its body and nibbling when the others weren't looking.

Then the mother bird flew away suddenly, and the boy realised he'd made a mistake. He should have stayed on the mother bird's back, so that when she flew down to the ground to catch some more dinner, he could jump off. But now he would have to wait for her to come back.

Just then the biggest chick asked, 'Where's that wiggly thing Mummy had on her back?'

'*Babykins* got it!' said the middle chick in a nasty voice.

'I didn't! I didn't! I got *nothing*! Waaaaahhhh…' wailed the littlest one.

'What was it?' asked the middle chick.

Babykins said, 'It was a *worm*!'

'No!' shouted the biggest chick. 'Don't be stupid. It had hair!'

'It was a worm wearing a wig!' Babykins whined.

'That's stupid, too!' shouted the middle chick. 'It was wearing *shoes*!'

'It was a worm… with a wig *and* shoes!' said Babykins sulkily.

'No!' said the biggest chick. 'Worms have only got one leg!'

Babykins began to cry. 'It was wearing both shoes on one foot!' it insisted.

Just then the middle chick exclaimed, 'Look! There it is! Up there! Get it! Get it!'

And the three chicks started leaping up at the boy, trying to snatch him off the ledge. When that didn't work, they tried another tactic.

'Come down, *please*,' said the biggest chick sweetly.

'No,' said the boy. 'You'll eat me.'

The middle chick said, 'Oh, we won't do that. We're *nice* little birds!'

'We just want to play with you…'

'Tell you stories…'

'Be your friend…'

The boy said, 'I don't trust you!'

Baby chick began to cry. '*Nobody* trusts me!' he whined.

The chicks whispered together for a while, and then the middle chick jumped onto the back of the big chick, and the littlest chick climbed onto the back of the middle chick…

'Now we're gonna show you a *good* game,' said the biggest chick sweetly.

'Yeah,' said the middle chick. 'We like this game.'

And Babykins screeched, 'It's called *Eat the Boy!*'

And he snapped at the boy's legs, ripping bits of his trousers off. The boy had nothing to defend himself with, except the book (which he still had in his jacket pocket). He took it out and began hitting the baby chick with it. But in a few moments, the book was snatched from his hand and the three chicks fell backwards into the nest.

The boy started crawling away before the birds could start on him again. He couldn't climb out of the cave, so he crawled further inside. Deeper and deeper and deeper…

Meanwhile, the baby bird was tearing the book to shreds and gobbling it down.

'There's nothing better than a good book!' he cheeped.

The boy stumbled deeper into the mountain, and soon the darkness was so great that he couldn't see his own muddy fingers in front of his face. This went on for hours: darkness, darkness and more darkness.

The cave got narrower and lower and soon he was crawling on hands and knees…

… across hard rock which scratched his hands…

… through cold, slimy, muddy patches where his arm would suddenly sink in, right up to his shoulder, and he would feel nasty, slithery things wriggling about deep in the mud…

'Home was never like this,' he said as he crawled along. 'At home I *never* had to crawl through pitch black tunnels or fight off hungry birds. They were actually very nice to me at home, most of the time. If I ever get home, I'll never run away again. I'll give my parents a big hug. And I'll even –'

But just then he looked up and saw a tiny speck of light.

'Look!' he cried out. 'It's not just a deep cave, it's a TUNNEL! It goes all the way to the other side of the mountain! I'm going to get out! I'm going to get home again!'

He started crawling faster and faster. And soon the tunnel opened out, so he could walk. Then the light grew, and he was able to run. Faster and faster he ran into the growing light, saying to himself as he ran:

'I'm going to make it! I'm going to get out! I'll be out of the tunnel, and then down the mountain, and back to my own house, and – and –

OH NO!'

He was *so* close. He could see the end of the tunnel, and the world just outside it. But between him and the mouth of the tunnel, there was a great crack in the floor.

It was about 3 metres wide.

He could never jump that! He looked left and right. He couldn't go around it, either.

He looked up. He couldn't climb up over it.

He looked down. 'I wonder if I could climb down, and then up the other side,' he said. He knelt at the edge and picked up a pebble. He dropped it into the chasm and waited, listening…

… and listened

    … and listened

… and listened.

And finally, there was a tiny *plink* from the some-where far, far below in the darkness.

'Right!' exclaimed the boy. 'I'm going to jump across!'

He carefully marked out his run-up and practised it several times. 'I can do this!' he kept telling him-self.

Finally he was ready. He started running. Faster he went, faster, faster. 'I can do it! I can do it!'

He came to the edge and jumped.

UP and UP and UP and ACROSS he went.

'I'm going to make it!' he shouted.

UP and ACROSS and DOWN he went… He was almost there!

DOWN and ACROSS and DOWN and DOWN… He was almost touching the other side!

'I'm going to make it! I'm going to –'

But just then an enormous arm came up out of the chasm, and a hand half as big as the boy himself grabbed the boy around the middle, and a big, booming voice said:

'COME 'ERE!'

The Trolls

The boy was pulled down into the chasm and across into a big cave lit by an enormous fireplace at the far end. A tall, ugly troll held the boy in front of his face and studied him closely.

'WHAT'VE YOU GOT, DEAR?' shouted the equally ugly mother troll, who was standing at the fire-place stirring a pot.

'IT'S A SPOIDER,' said the father troll.

'OH, *THEY'RE* TASTY! BRING HIM INTO THE KITCHEN AND PUT HIM IN THE POT!'

The father troll gave the boy a squeeze.

'WE GONNA EAT'CHA, SPOIDER,' he said.

'I'm not a spider! I'm a boy!' the boy exclaimed.

'NO, YOU AIN'T. BOYS ONLY GOT ONE LEG. I READ IT INNA BOOK.'

'But spiders have *eight* legs!'

'YEAH, BUT YOU MIGHT'VE LOST... LEMME SEE, EIGHT TAKE AWAY TWO... UH, YOU LOST FOUR LEGS.'

The mother troll shouted across, 'WHAT'S HE SAYIN'?'

'SEZ HE AIN'T A SPOIDER. SEZ HE'S A BOY!'

'CAN'T BE! BOYS HAS GOT THREE LEGS AND A LONG TAIL!'

The father troll shook his head. 'WE'LL HAVTA LOOK HIM UP IN DUH COOKBOOK.' He carried the boy further into the cave and took a huge, grease-stained book from a shelf.

'NOW LEMME SEE. SPOIDER... SPOIDER... HOW MANY "C"s ARE DERE IN SPOIDER, MY LOVE?'

'LOTS OF 'EM, DEAR.'

'HERE IT IS... NO, HE *AIN'T* A SPOIDER! LET'S LOOK UP "BOY". OOOOO, HE *IS* A BOY. LOOKS JUST LIKE DUH PICTURE. HUMANS IS *SO* UGLY! MAKES YUH FEEL SORRY FOR 'EM.'

The troll sadly shook his own cabbage-shaped head, making his ears flap and his potato-like nose wobble.

'LESSEE WHAT IT SAYS. FIRST, YOU GOTTA SKIN 'EM. LET ME GET MY SKINNIN' KNIFE...'

He picked up a long, sharp knife and poked the boy with it.

'GOTTA SKIN YUH. 'FRAID YOU AIN'T GONNA LIKE DAT. HUR HUR HUR...'

The troll laughed in the boy's face. Now, mountain trolls NEVER clean their teeth. This troll's teeth were green and slimy. They were full of holes, with large black worms crawling in and out of the holes.

'Oh, pooh!' said the boy. 'Don't you ever brush your teeth?'

'NAH, THAT'D RUIN 'EM. IT'D TAKE AWAY ALL DUH FLAVOUR!'

The troll looked back at the cookbook and read it

while dangling the boy from his large, rough hand. As he peered at the words one at a time (for he was very stupid), the oldest of his three children walked across to him. It was the girl troll. She whispered up to her father,

'DADDY, CAN I HAVE A BITE NOW? I'M VERY HUNGRY!'

'OF COURSE YOU CAN, MY PRINCESS. JUST ONE BITE THOUGH, YOU DON'T WANNA SPOIL YOUR DINNER.'

So the girl troll bit the part of the boy nearest to her teeth, which happened to be his trousers. She ripped one trouser leg off with her teeth and chewed it before swallowing it.

'HE'S VERY STRINGY, DADDY! HE GETS STUCK IN YOUR TEETH!'

The mother troll moved yet another enormous pot onto the cooker and shouted back, 'WE'LL HAVE TO BOIL HIM FOR A LONG TIME!'

'ROASTIN'S BEST,' said the father troll, still reading his book. 'GONNA ROAST YUH *HARD*,' he said to the boy. 'FRAID YOU AIN'T GONNA LIKE DAT, NEITHER. HUR HUR!'

Then the boy troll came up and asked, 'DADDY, CAN I HAVE A BITE, TOO? I'M STARVING!'

'YEAH, GO AHEAD, MY BOY. JUST LEAVE SOME FOR YOUR OLD DAD.'

The boy troll wasn't as tall as his sister, so he had to stand on tiptoe. And even then he could only reach the boy's feet. So he bit off one of the boys shoes and sat chewing it for a long time.

'HE'S VERY DIRTY AND CHEWY!' he complained.

'SLOW... ROAST...' read the father troll, 'IS BEST FOR... BOYS... 'CAUSE... THEY'RE... UH, T-T-T... TOUGHER THAN GIRLS. YEAH, DAT'S WHAT WE'LL DO.'

And now the baby troll crawled over and called up to its father, 'BITE! BITE!'

His father said, 'YEAH, YOU HAVE A BITE TOO, BABY.'

But the baby troll couldn't reach any part of the boy, so he bit his father's toe instead.

'BITE!'

'YOWWWWW! YOU STOOPID BABY!'

After a little more reading, the father troll shouted back to his wife, 'IT SEZ 'ERE DAT SOME BOYS IS POIS'NOUS!'

'WHICH ONES?'

'IT SEZ YOU CAN'T KNOW TILL AFTER YOU'VE EATEN 'EM!'

'OOOOO. THAT'S A BIT TOO LATE, INNIT? WE'LL HAVETA THROW HIM AWAY. DROP HIM DOWN THE HOLE, DEAR.'

The troll looked at the boy. 'WE GOTTA FROW YOU 'WAY. GONNA PUT YUH DOWN DE CRACK. *WEEEEEEEEEEE... SPLAT!* 'FRAID YOU AIN'T GONNA LIKE DAT. HUR HUR HUR!'

The boy thought quickly. 'But you don't have to do that!' he said.

'WHY NOT?'

'Because I know magic. I can teach you a magic *spell*!'

'I ALREADY KNOW HOWTA SPELL MAGIC. M – C – G – N – K – UHHH – ANOTHER C –'

'No! A magical spell which will turn me from a poisonous boy into a non-poisonous one!'

'WHY?'

'Because *then* you can eat me!'

'OH… YEAH… DAT'D BE A GOOD IDEA.'

The mother troll shouted, 'HOW'D YOU DO A SPELL? SHOW US!'

The father troll brought the boy into the kitchen and put him down.

The boy said, 'First you have to learn the spell by heart. All of you. Even the baby.'

'DAT'S ALL RIGHT. DUH BABY'S DUH CLEVER ONE OF DUH FAMILY.'

'You all have to stand in a line and repeat after me: Slipslog on a pognog…'

    'SLIPSLOG ONNA POGNOG'

'Wurzy dingle flopdoodle'

    'WURZY DINGLE FLOPDOODLE'

'Crogsnogger schluk chog'

    'CROGSNOGGER SCHLUK CHOG'

'Slimy grimy slurby woodle'

    'SLIMY GRIMY SLURBY WOODLE'

… On and on the spell went. It took hours to teach it to the trolls, because they were incredibly stupid. Finally, they could all say it by heart.

'Okay,' said the boy. 'Now I want you to all stand side by side in a line *just here*. You must put your legs together like *this*, and clasp your hands behind your backs like *this*.

'DAT'S VERY DIFFICULT,' said the father troll. 'DOIN' HANDS BEHIND DUH BACK. YOU CAN'T SEE DEM!'

'Sorry. But you *must* try. Then you have to close

your eyes and say the spell through all together. You must get it right, and keep your eyes shut for the whole spell, or else the spell will go wrong and you'll all be turned into... um, into something scary.'

'BALLET DANCERS,' said the father troll.

'DIRTY TEASPOONS,' said the mother with a whimper.

'PORRIDGE,' whispered the girl troll.

'SCHOOL SONGS!' said the boy troll nervously.

'BITE! BITE! BITE!' said the baby.

So they stood in line, closed their eyes and started the spell:
'SLIPSLOG ONNA POGNOG
WURZY DINGLE FLOPDOODLE
CROGSNOGGER SCHLUK CHOG
SLIMY GRIMY SLURBY WOODLE...'

And while they were reciting this long, long spell, the boy got some rope and tied all their legs together, and then their hands - all except for the baby, who couldn't do much harm except bite your toes. And then...

⌘ He dragged a pot full of steaming milk from next to the stove and put it in front of the father troll.

⌘ He pulled over a pot of hot bean soup and put it in front of the mother troll.

⌘ The girl troll got an enormous bowl of yesterday's custard, thick and yellow and very cold.

⌘ The boy troll got a huge bowl of yesterday's porridge, all cold and hard and slippery.

⌘ Lastly, he found a bowl which he filled with golden syrup and put it in front of the baby.

Then he tiptoed away to the edge of the kitchen and got ready to climb out of the cave. But he waited to see what happened.

The trolls finished their spell:

'OH WHIRLY KRIMBLE!
OH SLOPPY GROTSNUDDLE!
IN CUMBERPOT FULLSPIDDLE,
AMEN!'

The trolls opened their eyes. The boy waved to them. 'Tricked you!' he said. 'Byeeeee!'

The father troll roared, 'HE'S TRICKED US! AFTER HIM!' And he tried to take a step forward, but since his legs and arms were tied, he fell over…

…straight into the pot of steaming milk!

'OH NO! I HATE MILK! IT'S DISGUSTIN'!' he bubbled. But he couldn't get his head up, so he had to drink his way out. 'SLURRRRRP SLURRRRRP OH HORRIBLE… SLURRRRP… ARRRRR! OWW! IT BURNS ALL DUH WAY DOWN!'

His wife said, 'DON'T WORRY DEAR! I'LL GET HIM!' She tried to step forward….

… and fell headfirst into the pot of hot bean soup!

'NOT THE BEANS!' she screamed. 'THEY GIVE ME GAS!' But she had to eat her way out, sucking up all the soup. 'SSSSSSSSP! SSSSSSSSSP! OH I DON'T LIKE THISSSSSSSP! THE BEANSSSSSP GET SSSSSPTUCK UP MY NOSE!'

Meanwhile the girl troll was looking at her bowl of yesterday's custard. 'I'M GOING TO FALL INTO A BOWL OF CUSTARD!' she said brightly. 'BUT I HAVEN'T YET! … I'M GOING TO FALL INTO A BOWL OF CUSTARD… REALLY I AM… I AM! … BUT I *STILL* HAVEN'T!'

'Go on,' said the boy. 'At least it's not porridge.'

'OKAY!' And she threw herself into the custard and started sucking it all up.

The boy troll was laughing at his mother. 'YOU LOOK SO STUPID, MUM, WITH YOUR HEAD IN A POT OF BEANS AND YOUR BIG BUM STICKING OUT THE TOP! HEE HURR HEE HURR HEE – '

But he laughed so hard that he lost his balance and fell into the bowl of yesterday's porridge. 'OH YUK! IT'S COLD AND SLIMY! AND IT GETS IN MY EARS!'

That just left the baby, which climbed into its bowl of golden syrup and began swimming around in it happily. Then a thought occurred to it.

It climbed out and dragged the bowl over to where the father troll's legs hung out of the pot of milk, with his big feet dangling near the floor. The baby said to itself, 'NICE!' Then it got some golden syrup on its hands, and spread it all over its daddy's toes.

'WHAT'RE YOU DOIN', STOOPID BABY? DAT

TICKLES!'

The baby looked up at the toes dripping with syrup and said, 'NICE! BITE! BITE!'

And it bit the toes as hard as it could.

'YOWWWW! YOU STOOPID BABY!'

Homecoming

The boy was able to climb up from the troll's cave to the mouth of the big tunnel. Then he started running down the mountainside. After a while, he fell over and rolled down the mountainside instead. And then he landed on a piece of rock shaped like an enormous saucer, and it slid down the mountainside at a very frightening speed.

'Yippeeeee!' he shouted. 'I'm on my way home! Home! Hoooooooooooommmmmmmmme!'

The last "home" was so long because just then the saucer reached the end of the mountain and shot off through the air... and fell a long way... and landed in a river.

The rock saucer sank to the bottom, leaving the boy floating downstream very fast indeed. Soon he came to a village.

'I know this place!' he cried. 'This is *my* village! I live here!' So he swam to the bank and climbed out.

He started running through the streets. He was stained all over with mud, had only one shoe, and was missing most of his trousers, but he didn't mind. He waved at everyone he passed, and kept running.

'This is my street!' he shouted as he turned a corner. 'And there's the gate to my house!'

He jumped over the gate and ran up the path. The door was open, and he ran inside.

It was suppertime, and the family were sitting down to a very sad dinner in the kitchen. There was even a place set for the boy, though they thought he must be gone forever.

He burst into the kitchen and shouted, 'I'M BACK! And I'm NEVER going to run away again! Oh yes, I'm SO glad I don't have to eat beetles and worms, and fight off huge, hungry birds, and escape from horrible trolls! From now on, I'm going to be nicer to you all. I'll even kiss my little sister…'

He looked at his baby sister, who had jam spread all over her face and both her hands. She opened her arms wide and puckered up her jam-covered lips for a big, sticky kiss.

'I'll even kiss my little sister…

… TOMORROW!'

The Pink Pig

The voices

Rose the Pink Pig speaks rather primly for a pig. You can tell from her voice that she's quite a shy child who would love to run about laughing and shouting and getting covered with mud, but doesn't know how to begin. She covers up her shyness in front of her brothers and sisters by putting on airs and pretending to herself that she's better than them.

Her Mother sounds like any sensible mother anywhere, but in a thoroughly piggy manner.

Her Brothers and Sisters play rough, look rough, sound rough and when the wind is in the wrong direction, they smell rough, too.

The Wolf has a wonderful voice: so soft, so rich, so well-educated. In his spare time he does audio tapes of romantic novels, which housewives over the age of 40 listen to, while sighing a lot. As soon as he opens his mouth, you *know* that he's someone you can trust... though the rows of long, sharp teeth ought to warn you otherwise. His singing is beautiful, and he dances the Waltz and the Foxtrot quite divinely.

The story

Once upon a time, a tiny girl piglet was born, the colour of strawberry bubble gum.

Mother Pig asked her, 'And who are *you*, my little pink wriggler?'

'I'm your dear little piglet,' the Pink Pig replied.

Her mother teased her, saying, 'Oh no, you are *quite* the wrong colour for a piglet. I think you are... a tomato!'

'But I have a pig nose - and a pig tail - and pig trotters - and - and – waaaah!' the piglet cried. 'Look - I even have pig tears!'

'Yes, you're right,' said her mother kindly. 'I'm sorry I teased you. Let's see... I think I will call you *Rose*. Come have some milk, little Rose.'

But this was just the beginning. Her seven brothers and sisters started teasing her, too. When she wriggled in to get her share of milk, one of them asked:

'And what are YOU?'

'I'm your lovely little sister!' she announced.
'No you're not. You're a fire engine!'
'You're a letter box!'
'You're a telephone kiosk!'
'Fire engine! Nee nah nee nah nee nah!'
'I think she's a strawberry.'
'Nah, she smells like cherry mouthwash!'

Rose was offended. 'Well,' she said, '*you* lot are dirty and disgusting! You're *slobs*!'
'No, we ain't. We's pigs.'
'Yeah. Pigs always look dirty and smell a bit stinky.'
'Except you!'
'Fire engine! Ha ha!'

And because they were mean to her, she was mean back. She called them stinkytoes and mushfaces and slobberchops. And she became very particular about keeping clean:

🐖 She always walked around mud puddles, whereas her sisters splashed in them and her brothers swam in them.

🐖 She always drank her water neatly from the water tank, whereas her sisters splashed one another with it and her brothers swam in it.

🐖 She always ate her "slops" very carefully from the trough, whereas her sisters splashed their whole heads in it and her brothers jumped in the trough and swam in it.

'You lot are most dreadfully *dirty*,' she would sniff.

'Oh yeah?' they would reply. 'Well, YOU is most dreadfully clean!'

'At least WE ain't gonna be mistaken for a cherry tomato!'

'Yeah!'

And they all chanted: 'Cher-ry! Cher-ry! Cher-ry!', as if she was one of those sad Reality TV presenters.

'You don't love me!' she cried.

'Yeah, dat's right, we don't love you 'cause you ain't really a pig. You's just a washin' machine wiv legs!'

'I'm going to run away!' she said, for the tenth time that week.

'Yeah? Make sure you run somewhere clean, then! Ha ha!'

The Escape

Running away was going to be difficult. She was in a close-boarded pigpen, and the gate was always firmly locked. But after a few weeks of being teased so unkindly, she decided she *must* escape.

For days she searched the pigpen, prodding and pulling at the boards. Finally she found one that was loose and spent a morning working it even looser.

As she was getting ready for the final push, there was a thunderstorm. She ran back into the little shed, while her sisters all ran out the other way and started splashing in the rain, and then her brothers pushed past her, dived into the puddles and swam about in them.

Finally the skies cleared and the Pink Pig tiptoed around the puddles back to her board. She prised it off and skedaddled out of sight, carefully avoiding a monstrous puddle just outside.

You must remember that puddle. It's important later on...

She ran across a grassy field and into a dense wood. She followed a narrow path through the trees and came to a place where the path forked. She stopped and looked both ways.

An animal stepped out from behind a tree. It looked like a large grey dog. It had great white teeth, yellow eyes, and a dark red tongue. The teeth looked very sharp.

'Ahh... a little pig!' it exclaimed softly, in a rich, cultured voice. 'Without a doubt the loveliest, pinkest, sweetest little morsel that I have ever been blessed to see... good morning, my little friend.'

It licked its lips with its long red tongue.

Rose the Pink Pig knew she shouldn't talk to strangers. But this animal was behaving so wonderfully... It didn't tease her! It was *nice* to her! And it spoke so beautifully, in a voice that was musical, gentle and low.

It was speaking now. It said smoothly, 'I was just thinking what a gorgeous day it is. And now my pleasure is doubled by sharing this lovely day with such a fine, glowing example of pigginess.'

Rose asked shyly, 'Are you fond of pigs? Even pink ones?'

The animal nodded its grey, noble head. 'Especially pink ones,' it said. 'To me, a pink pig is as sweet as... a lollipop.'

'Truly?' she asked with a happy sigh.

'Truly, my dear little piglet. But tell me: why are you here, my pretty pink friend?'

'I've… I've run away.'

'Ah yes. I can see you're a strong, independent type. An explorer. A maverick. One who answers The Call of the Wild.'

'Me?' She didn't know what a maverick was, but it sounded good.

'Yes *you*, dear little piglet.' The animal licked its lips again. 'And might I add that you're *just* the sort of deliciously adventurous guest that my children would love to see!'

'What? Someone wants to see *me*?' she asked, not believing her pink, piggy ears.

'Indeed. You see, I have some lonely little children at home, and they would love to eat you – ah, I mean *meet* you. We should so like to have you for dinner – I mean, *to* dinner.'

It licked its lips again, showing its sharp teeth.

Poor animal, thought the Pink Pig. *He must have very sore lips. That's why he keeps licking them…*

She said out loud with a great sigh, 'I would love to come. But what kind of animal are you? My mother's told me the names of some of the animals, but she hasn't mentioned *anyone* like you!'

The animal bowed very politely. (*What wonderful manners he had!*). He said, 'I am a Wol– um, a *Wooffle*.'

The Pink Pig wrinkled her piggy nose. 'A Wooffle?' she asked. 'I've never heard of one of *them* before!'

'Oh, your mother and father know me very well indeed. We Wooffles have a long tradition of dropping by pigpens for a quick snack. I was thinking just the other day how pleasant it would be to invite you all to my house…'

The Pink Pig looked into the Wooffle's lovely yellow eyes. He had such a kind voice, and said such nice things! *And* he knew her mother and father.

She said, 'I'm very pleased to meet you, Mr Wooffle. But I don't know if I'm allowed to visit you. Maybe I should go home and ask my mother.'

The Wooffle looked very sad. He gave a great sigh and said in his beautiful voice, 'That is such a pity. I have some unusually sticky sweets and prodigiously succulent chocolates which I was saving for today... but if you cannot come, I shall have to throw them to the birds (*sigh*).'

'What a waste!' squealed Rose.

'And then of course there are the cream cakes and the bowls of buttery popcorn; the nut-topped ice cream; spicy crisps; black forest gateau; trifles of thick creaminess and sherry richness —'

'STOP!' the piglet shouted desperately. 'I'll come!'

'Very good,' said the Wooffle.

Rose sighed. 'After all,' she said, 'it's just the sort of food my mother and father like, too.'

So they rose and took the left hand fork, deeper into the woods and up a gentle slope.

Wooffle Manor

The Wooffle's house was built into the side of a hill just within the shadow of the woods, with its windows looking out over a pleasant garden.

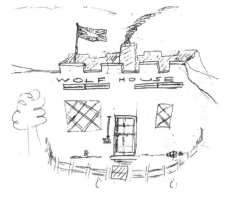

The Pink Pig followed the Wooffle inside, still wondering if this was the right thing to do.

The Wooffle said, 'I'm afraid my little children aren't home just yet. They're at Sunday School, praying for adventurous piglets. They'll be so pleased to see you. They haven't had a pig for lunch – um – I mean a pig to lunch – for a long time.'

The main room just inside the door was a kitchen. From the overhead beams were hanging pans and pots and skewers and skillets and food.

The piglet walked around in dizzy circles, looking up at everything. She saw something long and reddish brown hanging down from a hook. It looked like a long, fat sausage.

'What's that?' she asked the Wooffle.

'That's a salami,' he said.

'Oh. What's it made of?'

'It's made out of pig– I mean, *pigeons*.'

'Oh. I thought salami was made out of pigs.'

'Did you? What an odd idea.'

And what about that funny pie on the table?'

'That's a pork – ah, I mean a *porcupine* pie.'

'Wouldn't that be a bit prickly?'

'Yes,' said the Wooffle sadly. 'They aren't particularly tasty.'

The Pink Pig noticed something else on the table. Something round and covered with breadcrumbs. 'Is that an *eyeball*?' she squealed.

'No. It's a Scotch Egg.'

'I know them! They're made out of pigs!'

'No, little piglet. They're – ah – eggs laid by special Scottish chickens.'

'Oh. Really?'

'Undoubtedly.'

As he was talking, the Wooffle filled a pot with water and put it on the stove. It was a huge pot. It was larger than the piglet!

He added salt and pepper to the pot. 'Are you sad about being pink?' he asked.

'Very sad,' she said. 'Everyone's so mean to me!'

'How kind of you to tell me,' said the Wooffle. 'And how *wise* you are to trust me! You see, I can help you...'

'Can you?'

'Yes! In this pot I will place a little magic potion which will turn you a normal colour.' He licked his lips again as he took a pinch of herbs from a jar.

'Sage and thyme and a secret ingredient... And now all *you* have to do is hop in!'

'And it will work?'

'Assuredly so. It will be the end of all your troubles...'

'It's not too hot?'

The Wooffle raised the lid and dipped one hairy forepaw into the water.

'Yiiii!' He dropped the lid back onto the pot and danced about the room, shaking his paw. 'Er – no,' he said with a groan. 'It's a *lovely* temperature. Just right for a little swim!'

'All right then,' said the Pink Pig. 'I'll try *anything*!'

The Wooffle picked up the pig in his great, furry paws and carried her over to the stove.

'Soon you won't worry about your colour ever again,' he

promised.

'How lovely!' she exclaimed.

The Wooffle took off the pot lid again. Steam rose from the water and swirled around the piglet.

'Now, in we go –' he began.

But just at that moment, the doorbell rang five times and the door was banged open. He dropped the pot lid onto his foot.

'Drat!' he exclaimed.

In rushed his five small, furry children. He turned to shout at them and bashed the pot with his elbow.

'Tarnation!' he cried, and dropped the piglet, who went rolling across the floor. She collided with the five children and they bounced about the room, one of them landing up against the legs of their furious father.

He fell backward and knocked the pot onto the floor. The hot water sizzled about his furry toes.

'YEOWW!' he shouted. He slipped over and fell into the scalding water. And then he howled, a long, rising howl which told the piglet exactly what he was:

A WOLF!

The Return

The Pink Pig dashed for the door. The Wolf raised his head from the floor and howled to his wolf cubs:

'AFTER HERRRRRRRR!'

As the Pink Pig raced through the garden, all six wolves ran at the door together and got stuck in it. They howled and pushed and squeezed and pushed and howled… and finally it broke, and they all tumbled into the front yard in a tangled, howling heap.

The pig squealed and ran faster – so much faster that she tripped and rolled down the hill. The wolves hurled themselves down the hill after her.

She tried to climb a tree but then remembered – 'Pigs can't climb!'

'Faster!' howled the Wolf. And his five wolflings howled:

'Faster! Faster! Faster! Faster! Faster!'

She jumped in the air and tried to fly but remembered – 'Pigs can't fly!'

('Faster!' howled the Wolf. And his five wolflings howled: 'Faster! Faster! Faster! Faster! Faster!')

Finally the pig ran and bounced and rolled to the bottom of the hill. In front of her was that huge, muddy puddle – 'Oh, no, I can't swim!'

('Faster!' howled the Wolf. And his five wolflings howled: 'Faster! Faster! Faster! Faster! Faster!')

The wolves were nearly upon her, and it was too late to swerve around the puddle. So she leapt into it, expecting to sink like an enormous pink stone…

…But of course pigs were made to wallow through mud. And SPLOSH and SQUELCH and SQUISH she surged into the deep, rich, chocolatey mud…

…Then SLURGE and SLIPSLITHER and SLURM-SLOP she cut right through the middle of it, like swimming through toffee ice-cream, thicker than black treacle, more slippery than egg custard, more lovely than a Christmas pudding.

But wolves are not made for mud.

SPLUT!
    went the father wolf into the puddle.
Splut! Splut! Splut! Splut! Splut!
    went the five wolf cubs.
'Oh, Blast!' exclaimed the Wolf.
'Blast! Blast! Blast! Blast! Blast!' exclaimed his children.

The wolves were coated with heavy, black, cold mud. They could scarcely move.

Slowly, and with many a howling curse, the father

wolf crawled out and then pulled his children free. They skulked away to the shops and bought sausages for lunch instead.

Meanwhile, Rose the Pink Pig wallowed home.

'Hello Mummy, I'm back!' she exclaimed cheerily.

'Oh really, dear?' asked her mother. 'Have you been somewhere?'

'Yes, Mummy, and it was *horrible!*'

'Ah well, it's dinner time. The trough is full of lovely slops, so get stuck in!'

Rose was very hungry after her frightening experience, and threw herself at the food. Surprisingly, her brothers and sisters were delighted to see her.

'You look great!' one of them said.

'Yeah, like a big mud pie!'

'Pukka pong, Rose.'

'So smelly **and** gooey.'

'Dee-licious, sis!'

'A rose by any other name would still smell as sweet... I read dat in a book I ate yesterday.'

'You stink reeeeal good!'

As for being pink, it was never a problem after that, because no one could see it under all the mud!

The Gorilla

The voices

Ernest the Gorilla is clever, cool and rather geeky. He talks in a lively manner – as if he's selling bananas on a market stall. He's always polite and finds life very amusing... even when it's also very dangerous.

His mother has quite a loud voice, especially when she's shouting at Ernest.

The Crocodile has to do most of his talking with a gorilla clenched between his teeth, but you can tell from his voice that he's an ordinary sort of guy who would worry about whether his trousers matched his shirt, if he wore either. He's rather like your Deputy Headteacher.

The King of the Jungle speaks with a posh accent. He's not the cleverest animal you'll ever meet, and can get quite agitated about the tiniest thing. If you have a Great-Uncle Charles who wears a moustache and was an Officer in some war long ago, that's just what the Lion sounds like. Or maybe like Captain Mainwaring from Dad's Army.

The Lion's Wife – the lioness – is a calm, intelligent lady who puts up with a lot.

The Hyena has a screeching, irritating voice. Almost a howl at times. Try making the sound *nyeh-ha-haaaa!* in the back of your nose and you'll get the idea. She's the sort of female who would talk and talk and talk to you loudly in an annoying fashion about something totally unimportant like her latest pair of shoes, until you run from the room.

The story

Once upon a time, there was a gorilla named Ernest. He woke up one morning, went downstairs and had breakfast (a banana) and was just about to go back to bed when his mother shouted down the tree:

'Ernest! Time to go to school!'

'But Mum – school's a dangerous place… '

'No arguing! Off to school with you!'

So off he went down the path that led through the jungle to the gorilla school. But as he passed near to a deep, dark river, out from the river leapt a long, green animal with a lot of very sharp teeth.

A CROCODILE!

And the crocodile dragged the gorilla into the river, congratulating itself:

'Oh goody! A nifes liffle guwilla for bweakfast!' (He had to talk like that because he had a gorilla in his mouth).

But Ernest was a very clever gorilla, so he said to

the crocodile:

'You haven't brushed your teeth today, have you?'

And the crocodile said, 'Waff you mean, I haven't bruffed my teefs?'

'Well,' said Ernest, 'if you don't brush your teeth, your breath starts to smell. *Your* breath smells just like stinky fish! And *that* means the lady crocodiles won't kiss you!'

'Ooh… thaffs not nifes!'

'Ah, but it gets *worse*! If you don't brush your teeth, you have to go see the Crocodile Dentist. And he pokes about in your mouth with his Crocodile Teeth Pokers, and *then* he gives you a BIG injection. And for crocodiles, the needles are *that* long!'

Ernest held his paws wide apart. 'And he sticks the needle DEEP into your jaw like this – *whump!* – and fills it full of nasty stuff – *squidge squidge squidge…*'

'Ooh, thaffs not nifes either!'

'Ah, but it gets *worse*! If you don't brush your teeth, the Crocodile Dentist has to drill holes in them. So he gets out his Crocodile Drill – and for crocodiles, the drills are THAT big – and he pushes it onto one of your rotten teeth and goes NEEEE NEEEEE NEEEEEEEEEE!'

Ernest made the sounds of a huge machine drilling through a wall.

'Oh no!!!'

'Ah, but it gets *worse*! If you don't brush your teeth, sometimes the Crocodile Dentist has to pull them out! And he gets his BIG Crocodile Tooth Pliers and he STICKS them in your mouth and CLAMPS them onto a bad tooth and goes *scrrnch SCCRRRNCH*

SCCCCCRRRRRNCHCHCHCH.... POP!'

The crocodile cried out, 'OH NO! How howwible! Oh, *please* tell me how to stop that happening!'

'I know!' said the gorilla, 'I'll show you how to brush your teeth!'

'Would you? Oh *please* show me how!'

'Of course. Not a problem. You just swim me over to the river bank and let me go, and I'll show you.'

So the crocodile took the gorilla back to the river bank and released him.

The gorilla said, 'Okay, first of all, open your mouth nice and wide... that's right... now I'll just find some toothpaste...'

And he reached down and dug out some slimy, smelly mud and spread it in the crocodile's mouth.

'That taftes diffgufting!' said the crocodile (he had to talk like *that* because his mouth was full of mud).

'All toothpaste tastes disgusting,' said Ernest. 'Now let me find a good toothbrush...'

And hunted about until he found a big stick, as big as he was himself. He took it back to the crocodile and said,' Now keep your mouth open wide...'

He raised the stick high over his head and then brought it down as hard as he could, right onto the crocodile's bottom teeth...

WHACK!

'*Oooh!!!* Fank you fery much...' said the crocodile.

'You're welcome,' said Ernest the gorilla. 'I'll come back tomorrow and give you another lesson.'

The Second Trip

So Ernest went home and had a second breakfast (bananas again, of course). But as he was finishing the last bite, his mother came downstairs from sweeping the tree branches and said:

'Ernest! What are *you* doing here?'

'Well, Mum, it's like this. School is a dangerous place. This morning, there was a river and –'

'Ernest! Go to school!'

'Yes, Mum.'

He set off again down the path and then along the river (where the crocodile was showing the other crocodiles how to brush their teeth). He left the river and was walking next to a broad grassy space, when across the grass came bounding a large golden beast with a great shaggy mane and posh accent:

A LION!

The lion grabbed the gorilla by a leg and dragged him into the grassy clearing, boasting to himself:

'The King of the Jungle captures a crunchy little gorilla for breakfast! Ha ha, little gorilla! Prepare - to - DIE!'

But Ernest just put his fingers to his lips and went, 'SHHHHH!'

'What?' cried the lion indignantly. 'Whatcha mean, PVSSHHHH? You don't say PVSSHHHH to the King of the Jungle!'

'*Quiet!*' whispered Ernest. 'He might hear us!'

'What? Who?'

'The Hunter!'

'Hunter? Where? Where?'

'Get down! He's looking this way!'

And the lion dropped to the ground and covered his head with his paws.

Ernest whispered, 'He's just over there – no, don't look up, he might see you! Yes, he's just behind that tree. And… OH NO!'

The lion asked in a shaky voice, 'What is it?'

'He's got a LION GUN!'

'He has?'

'Yes! And you know about lion guns, don't you?'

'Uh… yes, yes, of course I do… I'm the *King of the Jungle!*'

'Lion guns are *this* long!' Ernest spread his arms very wide. 'And the bullets are *this* BIG!' He held his paws apart, fingers just touching, as if he was holding a grapefruit.

The lion groaned, 'Oh no… lion gun… bullets *that* big… I'm going to die!'

'Look,' said Ernest. 'I'd like to help you out. I mean, you're the King, right? So what I'll do is this: you let me go, and I'll creep up *around* the hunter and lure him away into the forest.'

'Yes,' said the lion. 'You do that. You, um, lure him away. And then you'll come back here and be eaten, right?'

'Of course,' said Ernest. 'That's only fair.'

'You won't run away after you've saved me from the hunter, will you?'

'Would I try to escape from the King of the Beasts?'

'No, no, of course not!'

'Right. So keep your head down. Don't let the hunter see you… '

And Ernest crept away, climbed a banana tree and found a big banana. Then he crept back v-e-r-y quietly until he was standing just behind the lion's long, furry back. He stretched back the arm that was holding the banana and then he THREW it with all his might at the lion.

And as it hit the lion right in the middle of the back, he shouted:

'BANG!'

And the poor lion collapsed, moaning hoarsely to himself in a quaking voice, 'I've been shot! I've – been – *shot*! With a Lion Gun! And the bullets are *that* big! I'm dying! Me! The King of Beasts! *Dying!*'

So Ernest went home. But as soon as he put his paw on the front doorknob, his mother called out, 'Ernest! I hope that's not *you* coming home!'

'No, mum,' he said. 'It's not me.'

'Go to school!'

'School's a dangerous place, Mum. Even getting there is tricky. There's crocodiles and lions and –'

'Ernest!'

'Yes, Mum...'

... And the Third Trip

He headed off down the path again, past the river and past the grassy area where the lion was still lying on his side, moaning.

Just then, the lion's lady wife – the lioness – came bounding up to her husband.

'Hello, dear!' she said. 'Are you having a good morning?'

'NO, I'M DYING!' said the lion crossly. Then he added in a weak voice, 'Shot by a Lion Gun... the bullets are *that* big... I'm dying... oh, *why* does it take so long to die?'

The lioness asked, 'Are the bullets yellow, dear?'

'Of course not!'

'Are they shaped like a banana?'

'What?'

The lion looked behind him. Then he leapt up and began running up and down the little clearing, growling and spitting and complaining:

'I've been *tricked*! Me, the King of the Jungle, *tricked*

by a gorilla! Oh, if I catch that gorilla, death will be too good for him! I'll … I'll *pull his little paws off*!'

He pulled off imaginary gorilla paws, making a lot of bloodthirsty paw-pulling noises. '*Skeeerrreech – kkkrrrummmp!*'

'If I catch that pesky little gorilla, I will personally twist his head off! *Sccrnch, sccrrrrnnnnch, scccrrrop!*'

'If I catch that disrespectful gorilla, I will take my claws and RIP HIS SKIN OFF! Ha ha! *Shrrreeeeeeeee-rchhhh-schhhhrccchhh!*'

And so Ernest hurried off towards his school. This time he almost got there. But just as he was turning the final corner, something leapt out of the bushes.

Something a bit like a dog, but much uglier. Something with a big head and a lot of fur about the neck. Something with far too many teeth.

It was A HYENA.

Worse than that, it was a *lady* hyena.

'Nyyyyyaaahahahahaha!' the hyena screeched as she dragged the poor gorilla into the bushes. 'A niiiiice little gorilla for my morning snack! Okay, gorilla, *say your prayers!*'

But Ernest always said his prayers, so he was ready for anything a hyena could do. He looked the lady hyena in the eyes and said:

'It's *you*! I've been looking for you *everywhere!*'

The hyena was shocked. 'What?' she shrieked. 'Whaddya mean? NO ONE looks for a hyena!'

'Don't you know who I am?' asked Ernest.

'Yes!' she snapped. 'You're a tasty little gorilla!'

'But no... I'm a *hairdresser!*'

The hyena stared at him. 'A *what*?' she snarled.

'Don't you read the fashion magazines? Hyena's Weekly? Hyena Vogue? CosmoHyena?'

'Never heard of 'em!' she snapped.

'Well, I do the hair for all those celebrities in OK Hyena and Hyena Hello! But they all told me that your hair is THE BEST. And they were right! It's just sooooo gorgeous!'

The hyena put the gorilla down and stroked the dirty fur along her neck with a dirty forepaw. 'Well, I suppose it *is* rather nice,' she said. 'I try to look after myself. Bit of exercise, bit of pampering, eat the right things, you know. *Including* little gorillas!'

'Oh yes, of course! But before you eat me, can I do your hair for you? Just this once?'

'All right, then. I'll make you a deal, little gorilla. You do my hair. And *then* I'll eat you!'

'Of course. No problem!'

The gorilla fluffed some hair up and smoothed some down. He pulled bits out ('*yowwwwl!*') and got some mud and plastered it all over her head and then scraped some of it off with a stick.

'There, you look *lovely!*' he said. 'I'll just go get a mirror to show you how beautiful you look. I left it at home. Back in a minute...'

The hyena leapt up, snarling, 'Oh, no you don't! You can't fool a hyena!'

'What, *me* try and fool *you*? Would I do that? Look, why don't you just come with me down to the river and I'll show you your reflection in the water.'

'Yeah. And then I'll eat you.'

'Of course!'

As they were walking back towards the river, the gorilla said to the hyena, 'I ought to warn you. There's a Mad Lion about.'

'Mad Lion? Whaddya mean?'

'This Mad Lion hates hyenas. He says that if he catches a hyena, he'll *pull its little paws off!*

Ernest pulled off imaginary paws. '*Skeeerrreech – ummmp!*'

'Oooooo... *that's* not nice!' exclaimed the hyena.

Ernest added, 'The Mad Lion said if he catches a hyena, he will personally *twist its head off! Sccrnch, sccrrrrnnnnch, scccrrrop!*'

'That's *horrible!*' exclaimed the hyena.

'He said that if he catches a hyena, he will take his big claws and RIP ITS SKIN OFF! Ha! *Shrrreeeeeeeee-rchhhh schhhhrccchhh!*'

'Oh no!!!' squealed the hyena. 'So vulgar!'

'But it's all right,' said the gorilla. 'I don't suppose he's anywhere near here.'

Just then they came to the grassy clearing, where the lion was still running up and down, muttering to himself, 'That bad, bad, lion-tricking gorilla! If I catch him, ohhhhh I'll make him suffer! I'll –'

As he turned around, the lion saw the gorilla and the hyena. And the lion stopped, pointed at them, and roared:

'You! Stay where you are! It's *payback time!*'

'What? Me? No – I – ' shrieked the Hyena. 'Help!!!' And she turned tail and ran away as fast as she could, and was never seen in the jungle again.

But the gorilla just stood there as the angry lion came bounding across the clearing toward him. He tapped his foot to the latest jungle jive CD and pretended not to notice…

'NOW, little gorilla!' shouted the lion as he landed right in front of Ernest. 'You tricked me once! *Once* is all you get in the jungle! So now, little lion-tricking gorilla: PREPARE … TO … DIE!'

Ernest asked innocently, 'Who? Me? There must be some mistake. *Me* trick the King of the Beasts? A little gorilla like me?'

'What d'you mean?' asked the lion. 'Mistake? The King of the Jungle doesn't *make* mistakes. I know who you are. *You* tricked me!'

'Oh! I understand now!' exclaimed Ernest, putting his paw to his head as if he'd just thought of something. 'It must be my brother you want!'

'What?'

'My twin brother Frank. He's *always* tricking lions! I tell him not to, but he never listens! "Frank," I say, "if you try to trick the King of the Jungle, you're going to be sorry." But does he take my advice? No.'

'Oh,' said the lion. 'Twin brother, hey? And he's *bad*, is he?'

'*Very* bad. And always rude to lions.'

'Hmmm. I'm not sure about this,' said the lion. 'You look *just* like the pesky little gorilla I met this morning. But twins, you say? That might explain it.'

'I tell you what,' said Ernest. 'My tree is just around the corner from here. I'll go get my brother Frank. We'll stand here side by side, and if you think it was *Frank* who tricked you, you can eat Frank. But if you think it was *me* who tricked you, you can eat *me*. You can't lose!'

The lion glared at him suspiciously, and then a crafty look came into his eyes. 'That's a good idea,' he said. 'You go get your brother Frank. And don't you worry about being eaten. It's certainly *him* I'll eat, not you. I can tell a lion-tricker when I see one!'

So Ernest went home and had lunch (banana soup with banana bread).

And his mother asked, 'Did you have a good morning at school, dear?'

'I'm afraid I didn't get to school, Mum. You see, school is a dangerous place. It's a real jungle out there... '

Meanwhile, the lion was waiting patiently for the gorilla to come back with his twin brother. His lady wife came bounding up gracefully and asked:

'Been shot with any bananas recently, dear?'

'Hush!' said the lion gruffly. 'I'm waiting for that cheeky little gorilla. He thinks he's been clever, but I've tricked *him* this time!'

'How?'

'He's going to go home and bring back his twin brother. *He* thinks I'm going to choose between eating him and eating his brother, but oh no! I've *really* tricked him this time! *I'm* going to eat them BOTH!'

The lioness looked at her husband and sighed. She asked, 'And how long have you been waiting?'

'Oh, about an hour.'

'And how far is it from here to the gorilla's tree, dear?'

'Just around the corner. The gorilla said... um, he said... you know –'

A thoughtful look came into the lion's eyes. Then he roared:

'OH NO!
TRICKED AGAIN!'

Some other books by Ed Wicke for ages 9 and over...

AKAYZIA ADAMS AND THE MASTERDRAGON'S SECRET
A school visit to London Zoo causes Kazy Adams to swap the rough streets of East London for a an unusual new world – a world of magic, adventure and danger. And in Old Winsome's Academy, there's an ancient mystery to solve: the disappearance of nine pupils during the Headship of the Masterdragon Tharg, at the time of the Goblin Wars... *The first book in the series.*

AKAYZIA ADAMS AND THE MIRRORS OF DARKNESS
The second adventure of Akayzia Adams and her friends starts with one mirror and ends with another. In between, there are three worlds of magic, a squadron of werewitches, a fistful of trolls, and one annoying little lizard with a taste for chocolate. And in the Academy, there are thousands of spiders... some of them not actually spiders at all.

MATTIE AND THE HIGHWAYMEN
Recently orphaned and running away from her bullying aunt, 13-year-old Matilda Harris finds herself down in The Devil's Eyeball with an eccentric, well-spoken highwayman; his gang Lump, Stump, Pirate and Scarecrow; and two young "brats" who have escaped from the notorious Andover Workhouse. Oddly enough, she comes to enjoy it... *An exciting tale set in the 1840s.*

BULLIES
The only book in the world with a fairy who conducts anti-bully warfare using beetles, a snowman that talks in riddles, a school assembly taken by a talking bear, a little sister who starts a pirate mutiny at school and a boy who turns into a bird after Christmas lunch! A book that's serious about bullying. But *crazy* about everything else!

NICKLUS
Nicklus is a nine year old boy who hardly talks at all. Marlowe is a talking cat, the "coolest cat in England". They make an unusual team as they join forces to upset the clever plans of a rather mad scientist to destroy all the cats in England. They also need to find Nicklus' missing mother. But how?

Lightning Source UK Ltd.
Milton Keynes UK
UKOW07f0413201114

241871UK00001B/8/P